Anonymous

Memorial of Sarah Pugh. A tribute of respect from her

cousins

Anonymous

Memorial of Sarah Pugh. A tribute of respect from her cousins

ISBN/EAN: 9783337306441

Printed in Europe, USA, Canada, Australia, Japan

Cover: Foto ©Raphael Reischuk / pixelio.de

More available books at **www.hansebooks.com**

MEMORIAL

OF

SARAH PUGH.

A TRIBUTE OF RESPECT

FROM HER COUSINS.

———

PHILADELPHIA:

J. B. LIPPINCOTT COMPANY.

1888.

TEACHER and friend beloved! thy steadfast light
Shone o'er my youth like a fixed star of right
And truth and goodness.   Welcome as soft airs
That breathe upon and lift the weight of cares,
Thy gentle presence, thine illumined soul,
Into the homes of those who loved thee stole
As unobtrusively as spirits may
Who feel no hindrance of encumbering clay;
" Peace to this house!" beamed from thy friendly face,
And order, heaven's first law, possessed the place,
Whatever jarred and fretted ceased its din,
And restful quiet straightway entered in.
So passed thy life, a fair unruffled page,
Ruled by the still, small voice from youth to age.

S. W. P.

PREFACE.

THE life of Sarah Pugh, outlined in this memorial, resembled a quiet stream, which is traced by the verdure of its banks. The record is given chiefly in her language, from letters and private memoranda.

Decided, firm, and prompt in any course of action which her judgment and conscience approved, mild and unobtrusive in manner, unruffled by opposition or difficulty, with strong attachments to friends, she furnished an encouraging example of moral power.

CONTENTS.

MEMORIAL OF SARAH PUGH.

CHAPTER I.

EARLY LIFE.

A BEAUTIFUL and happy life closed on the first of the Eighth month, 1884, when Sarah Pugh passed from earth. Her guiding motives through life were love and duty.

> "She had that gift of patient tenderness
> Which, seeing right, can yet forget the wrong,
> And, strong itself to comfort and sustain,
> Yet leans with full unfaltering confidence
> On the Great Spirit that enriches all."

Sarah Pugh, the daughter of Jesse and Catharine Pugh, was born in Alexandria, Virginia, the sixth of the Tenth month, 1800. Her parents were members of the Society of Friends, descended from those of that faith who came to America from the Old World, in the early part of the eighteenth century, to escape religious persecution. At the decease of Sarah's father when in her third year, the family, composed of the mother and two children, moved to the home of her grandfather, Isaac Jackson, who lived in New Garden, Chester County, Pennsylvania.

Isaac Jackson was characterized by a strict sense of justice and benevolence. He labored actively to procure the manumission of the slaves throughout the Yearly Meeting of Friends held in Philadelphia; and a similar devotion to what she believed to be true was a marked trait in his grand-daughter from early life.

A few years later Catharine Pugh and family, joined by her sister, Phebe Jackson, established a home in Philadelphia, where the sisters engaged in dress and cloak making. Catharine Pugh possessed a remarkably serene, equable temper, combined with kindness and steady industry. Under the influence of this quiet household, conducted in the simplicity which in that day marked the domestic life of Friends, Sarah passed her early years,—a delicately-formed but healthy child. It was her privilege to spend a part of her summers among her New Garden relatives, who were ever ready to receive her as their guest, being, in the language of her aunt, "such a good little girl and made no trouble."

Promptness and punctuality constituted one phase of her character which deserves especial mention, as it was most conspicuous throughout her life. The prudent care of a judicious mother trained her in regular habits, and inculcated the necessity of temperance in all things as a requisite for the preservation of health.

In Sarah's twelfth year she became a pupil at West-town Boarding-School, an institution established under the direction of Philadelphia Yearly Meeting of Friends, where she remained two years. In after-life she spoke with pleasant recollections of these school-days, and of her teachers with affectionate interest.

In 1821, Sarah commenced teaching Friends' school

in a room in Twelfth Street Meeting-House. Under
the supervision of the Monthly Meeting she discharged
the duties of that position satisfactorily seven years,
resigning at the close of the summer term in 1828.

Until 1828, Sarah seemed devoted to the Friends
as a religious sect. During the distracting agitation
which resulted in a division of the Society she became
mentally exercised on the subject of religion, and on
the twenty-eighth anniversary of her birth expressed
her feelings and doubts in the following language:

10*th mo.*, 1828.—" I go to the meeting of worship.
I have always been accustomed to attend, hoping that
wherever the sincere-hearted are met there will be a
blessing.

" I go *not* to the meetings of business,—thinking
they are conducted on the principles of bigoted pro-
scription, instead of Christian love,—though those who
are engaged therein 'verily believe they are doing God
service.'

" I join not the ranks of the other party, for, however much I admire some of their principles, and love
many of their members, I am not a sectarian.

> 'If I am right, Thy grace impart
>   Still in the right to stay ;
>   If I am wrong, oh, teach my heart
>   To find that better way !'

" ' Do justly, love mercy, and walk humbly.' In
this we agree, and perhaps in little more. Yet is not
this sufficient? Men should be judged by actions, not
opinions; of this I am more and more convinced.
Why, in their judgment of the former, do most agree ;

in the latter, few?   Yes, but ten of us agree that that
man's doctrine is unsound, and will lead to bad actions,
and it is best to nip the evil in the bud.   So man's
erring reason has directed him, and to what has it not
led?—to the dungeon, the rack, and the *auto-da-fé.*   He
assumeth the judgment-seat of the Almighty.   Even
when opinions lead to actions, place the criminal if
possible in such a situation as to prevent the repetition
of the crime; this is all the punishment man has a
right to inflict.

"It is my serious opinion more evil has been done in
the world, and its Almighty Ruler more dishonored,
by those professing to act in his name, and by some
who really believed they were doing God service, than
by all the infidels and atheists.   Whom shall we pro-
nounce destitute of saving faith?   The Mohammedan
says the Christian, the Christian the Jew, the Jew the
Heathen; and if we subdivide them, we find the Otto-
man and the sect of Ali among the Moslems, the Phari-
see and Sadducee of the Jew, and among Christians the
Roman Catholic denounces the Protestant, the Trinitarian Protestant the Unitarian, and many of these the
Deist.   May we not believe with the apostle, 'That of
every nation, tongue, and people, they that fear God and
work righteousness will be accepted of him'?

"On 12th mo. 3d, 1828, my beloved cousin, Hannah
Lewis, was married, and as we had from childhood been
as sisters, this event was full of interest.   I shared
with her in her pleasant anticipations, for many of
them were connected with myself; but, in the Seventh
month, after an illness of three months she ceased to be
numbered with the living.   That I was able to be with

her, to share with her afflicted sister the mournful duty of attending her, and to witness the calmness and sweetness that hovered over her, is a source of great consolation to me. May her genuine worth, her constant solicitude for the comfort of those around her, be held in remembrance as an incitement to follow her in well-doing!"

In 1829 her memorandum states she established a school in Walnut Street, "assisted by my early and beloved friend, Rachel Peirce. The children who were placed under my care were particularly interesting; some of them remained with us for years, and between them and myself there grew up a mutual and lasting attachment. That objects so every way calculated to warm my heart and occupy my feelings were given to me was a source of constant satisfaction."

In 1831 the school was removed from Walnut to Cherry Street below Eleventh, in the second story of Jacob Peirce's commodious school-house (his boys' school was on the first floor). In these pleasant quarters Sarah and Rachel procured the assistance of Sarah Lewis, and the trio worked together in unity. The grounds in front, partly cultivated by the owner as a flower-garden, contained also a frame building furnished with simple gymnastic apparatus, which afforded opportunity for healthful exercise to the pupils during the hours of recreation.

Jacob Peirce, an intimate friend and the legal guardian of the young teacher, had the same excellent ways of governing and instructing the young. One of his pupils, Mr. Henry Carter, speaks of him and his method of teaching as follows:

2

"He was a handsome man with a pleasing manner. I soon found that the whole school was ruled by love, and the self-respect and sense of duty he had by his example developed in his pupils. We were good boys; we loved him and would not give him pain. I never heard him say an angry word or betray impatience with the dullest. He did not, that I recollect, ever sermonize or give a moral lecture. When he did reprove it was in such a kindly way, seeming to be grieved that there was need of correction.

"He frequently took us for walks in the country, also to Pratt's Gardens and Peale's Museum. On these occasions we wandered about at will or collected around him while he told us of the flowers, trees, stones, etc.

"He tried to awaken in us an interest in our studies, and taught us also to think.

"It was his kindly, patient, sympathetic manner that embalmed his memory in the hearts of his pupils."

The course of study in Sarah Pugh's school was limited to the English branches. Instruction was practical, thought was aroused and stimulated, no antagonisms introduced, no going up and down in classes. Study was pursued for the purpose of obtaining results and storing knowledge for practical use in life, not with the motive of surpassing others. Government, mild but firm, was imposed more by personal influence than by precept, the rules were few and simple, and obedience rendered from respect and love for the teachers. This was shown in many cases years after school-days were past. A number of the old pupils attended, at stated times, the conversational social sessions held in the school-room endeared by pleasant associations, some bringing their children.

Into this busy, earnest life came the mournful sighing of the captive. Though Sarah Pugh was opposed to slavery by intuition and education, she had taken no active part in any of the anti-slavery movements which at this time were exciting the country until George Thompson visited Philadelphia. George Thompson, an ex-member of the British Parliament, whose labors in England had materially promoted the abolition of slavery in the British West Indies, came to this country at the suggestion of W. L. Garrison, to aid in advocating publicly the doctrine of immediate and unconditional emancipation. He passed through several States, speaking in various places, and by his eloquence aroused many persons previously indifferent. He also encountered bitter hostility from the pro-slavery party.

In 1835 Sarah heard him give an address in Philadelphia, and was at once impressed so forcibly that she became from that time an earnest abolitionist, and soon after joined the Female Anti-Slavery Society, which was organized in 1834, remaining an active member until it disbanded in 1870, after the liberation of the slaves. Sarah continued teaching, while working in the anti-slavery cause : she also joined the American Anti-Slavery Society, organized in Philadelphia in 1833.

In 1837 Sarah went to New York to attend the first meeting of the American Women's Anti-Slavery Convention. She describes her journey and experience in a letter to a friend.

5th mo. 8th, 1837.—" About fifty delegates took the boat for New York. Our journey was pleasant; no

particular incident, except on the steamboat at dinner
the colored waiter removed a plate before E. J. Neall
had finished her dinner. One of the party requested
him to supply another, adding, ' My friend will not eat
your dessert, as I suppose it is not free produce.' The
waiter caught the idea instantly, and served us with
alacrity. Dinner finished, the steward was spoken
to. He said, ' I, too, am an abolitionist. I became
interested in the subject last summer, while attending Brother Tappan's Sunday-School with my people,'
looking round on some ten or twelve assistants. ' I
have never been so happy as since I became interested
in the cause. I mean to examine the subject of free
produce, and may be better provided next year.'

" We obtained comfortable accommodations at a private boarding-house, attended a committee meeting in
the evening, and at ten A.M. on the 9th repaired to the
Tabernacle, a church on Broadway, capable of seating
four thousand persons, where we found a crowded
house. The officers and leading advocates of the anti-
slavery cause were arranged on seats in full view of the
audience. Alvan Stewart, James G. Birney, Gerrit
Smith, Francis Jackson, and others, a cheering assem-
blage of noble-looking characters. Arthur Tappan,
President, a grave, dignified-looking person, called the
meeting to order. Elizur Wright, Jr., Secretary, read
an abstract from the annual report, and several letters
from interested persons who could not attend. The
reading of the remonstrance against slavery from Scotland to the American people, containing more than four
thousand signatures, made quite a sensation. The best
speakers were selected to support the resolutions, and

they spoke with enthusiasm. The meeting held from
ten A.M. till three P.M., and *this was the Anniversary.*
Subsequent sessions for the transaction of business were
held in the session-room of the church, which would
accommodate six to eight hundred people. These sit-
tings were continued through the week. Women were
not admitted as members.

"The first anti-slavery convention of *women* assembled in a church in the northern part of the city of
New York in 1837. The meeting was organized on
Lucretia Mott's motion to appoint Mary S. Parker
President and Anne Warren Weston Secretary. The
session was opened by reading a selection from Scrip-
ture and prayer. The credentials of delegates and
several letters addressed to the convention were read,
a committee of business appointed, etc. Adjourned to
meet the following afternoon.

"In the evening we attended a sale of anti-slavery
articles held in a room on Broadway. We were not
obliged to 'skulk in holes and corners;' the goods were
neatly prepared and handsomely arranged. At the
table for refreshments we were helped to lemonade. A
gentleman proffered payment to a large black woman
who served it; she said, 'I will attend to that,—receive
it from me.' 'Whom are we to thank for this kindness?' 'My Master,' looking upward. 'Through
whom has he sent it?' 'My name is Esther Lang.'
'How glad we are to know thee!' Then there were
handshakings and kindly greetings. This noble woman,
by her own earnings, had purchased the freedom of
eleven slaves.

"The following day attended the morning session of

the Young Men's Anti-Slavery Society; about one thousand present, among whom were Beriah Green, Alvan Stewart, J. G. Birney, and John Hopper, whom his brother Josiah called the great unlynched. He gave an account of the treatment he received in Savannah. There was earnest speaking by these young men.

"At the adjourned session of the women's meeting a number of resolutions were introduced, and discussed with ability that was cheering to hear. On the third day they held two sessions. We should have been famished had not our thoughtful colored friends brought us baskets of refreshments; they are a race worth saving. About one-tenth of our number were colored. They did not take part in the general business, but when the subject of Colonization was taken up they spoke with earnestness. They responded also upon prejudice against color. The convention adjourned at five P.M., to meet next year in Philadelphia. These meetings were conducted with much propriety and decision, and we feel we did some good."

The differences of opinion as to methods of work for the anti-slavery cause among the immediate emancipationists, the no-unionists, and the advocates of political measures, caused a want of harmonious action. Party spirit was aroused, some acted with heated zeal, and exhibited a lack of charity, toleration, and Christian forbearance. How Sarah passed through this ordeal without being warped from the direct line of duty is shown in her own words in a letter to a friend.

11*th mo.* 20*th*, 1837.—" With respect to this controversy, Whittier's first letter gives my views exactly in regard to what many of us have had to bear from

the Calvinistic writers of the party. I rarely read
Garrison's writings that I do not wish to alter some
expression. They appear egotistical, bitter. Yet so far
as I am able to judge, they are so only in appearance.
I think he is *not* puffed up, but is really humble, and
though severe, it is in love. This may seem like a de-
termination to see only good, but it is not so; it is only
an endeavor to be just.

" When the reply to the Appeal appeared, I did not
then suppose, what subsequent disclosures have proved,
that the appellants were actuated by hostility to Garrison, which they cloaked with a love for the anti-
slavery cause. Witness their hypocritical charges
against the free colored inhabitants of Boston. Could
any one who really loved the cause have acted as they
did in publicly accusing one of its most devoted cham-
pions before, in private, expressing disapprobation?
This should first have been done, and time allowed for
change, at whatever inconvenience. It could have been
done without delay, as they were constantly meeting
him as friends. I can find no excuse for them. It
would perhaps be best to let the subject rest.

" Alas for the news from Alton (the murder of Elijah
P. Lovejoy, which occurred 11th mo. 7th, 1837). Why
did they arm themselves? They trusted in the arm of
flesh, and what has it availed them?

' In the evil days before us,
    And the trials yet to come,'

may we be strengthened to hold fast our faith and con-
fidence in the principle of resisting not evil, which is

perfectly consistent with crying aloud to show the people their transgressions and the nation its sin !"

Sarah, at first, hesitated to endorse the use of the fair as a legitimate method of raising money to aid in carrying on the anti-slavery work.   She satisfied herself, after consideration, that if conducted properly, without using deception, the plan was as legitimate as commercial trade.   Thus, her own mind at ease, she began to work with zeal, and was one of the chief managers of the Philadelphia fair until the need for using it expired.

CHAPTER II.

PENNSYLVANIA HALL.

In 1838 a beautiful hall was erected on Sixth Street, Philadelphia, by the friends of freedom, to be devoted to the free discussion of slavery, and other social and moral questions.   Arrangements were made for a three days' dedication service.   Many persons from different sections of the country came to attend these meetings.

5th mo. 14th, 1838, at ten o'clock A.M., the saloon of the building was opened for an oration from David Paul Brown upon slavery.   The hall was crowded,—many persons gathered in the street that could not get admittance because there was not room.   In the after-meetings a disorderly disposition was displayed, occasionally stones were thrown against the windows; those inside were protected by the heavy blinds from the rattling glass; the disturbance increased until the howling was terrific. The mayor demanded the key at the close of the afternoon meeting of the third day, locked the door, and addressed the crowd with mild advice to keep the peace, leaving the mob "as his police." At dusk the rioters broke into the building, and in less than an hour only four blackened walls remained of the beautiful hall.

The Women's Anti-Slavery Convention, which was held in New York the year previous, and adjourned to Philadelphia, held their sessions in the hall until it was consumed. Other accommodations were closed against them. Sarah Pugh invited them to hold their last session in her school-room, with the approval of Jacob Peirce, the owner of the premises.

A memorable and beautiful occasion was this, that closed so abruptly that bright, auspicious beginning. Sarah was particularly occupied with the meetings of the convention. There was some earnest speaking, and a solemn dedication of themselves to the duty of continuing to labor in this field, however hard the service might be. None knew at what minute the howling mob, composed of hundreds of infuriated men, might break in upon *them*, for they were racing through the streets, hunting anti-slavery victims or other objects upon which to wreak their vengeance.

On prejudice against color Sarah speaks for herself, 12th mo. 24th, 1839: "One of the most important of our testimonies is that relative to prejudice against color. It strongly influences the hearts of otherwise good people, and, as they cannot fortify themselves with arguments, they talk of innate feelings, natural repugnance, etc. It grieves the heart to see pretensions so hollow,—we must, however, only pity them. How much injury they do to themselves by allowing this evil feeling to possess them ! How true it is, and how admirably just, that we cannot injure another, even in thought, but we ourselves suffer !"

12*th mo.* 31*st.*—" This fall I engaged in a new depart-ment, to me, of anti-slavery labor, circulating petitions to be presented to Congress and the State Legislature, for the abolition of slavery. I never undertook any-thing that was so entirely distasteful to me; but, as it is in many things, the anticipation was more than the reality. In our aristocratic district we were generally civilly received and heard, and as civilly refused with few words. We had many interesting conversations and opportunities for showing forth abolition truth."

CHAPTER III.

THE WORLD'S CONVENTION.

In 1839 the British and Foreign Anti-Slavery So-ciety called a general conference to meet in London on the 12th of June, 1840, " to deliberate on the best means of promoting the interests of the slave and bringing about his immediate and unconditional freedom ; and by every *pacific measure* to hasten the utter extinction of the slave-trade." To this conference "they earnestly invited the friends of the slave, of every nation and of every clime."

To this invitation the Massachusetts and Pennsylvania anti-slavery societies responded by appointing male and female delegates to attend the convention. Sarah Pugh, from the Philadelphia female society; James and Lucretia Mott, Abby Kimber, Henry and Mary Grew, and Elizabeth J. Neall, of Philadelphia; Isaac and Emily Winslow, Abby Southwick, and George Bradburn, of New England anti-slavery societies, embarked in the packet-ship " Roscoe," 5th mo. 7th, 1840.

Sarah Pugh writes describing her first ocean experience: "After severe gales, with the discomforts attending them, we have rejoiced every day, when able to be on deck. We never wearied of the grandeur and magnificence spread out before us. All the descriptions we had read, all the epithets of glory, beauty, might, and boundlessness, seemed realized to our charmed vision." They landed at Liverpool and proceeded to London, stopping at Chester, Manchester, Birmingham, Warwick, Kenilworth, Stratford-on-Avon, Woodstock, and Windsor, reaching London on the 5th of 6th mo., 1840.

"Joseph Sturge breakfasted with us at our boardinghouse on the 6th. He was pleasant and gentlemanly, and disposed to be friendly,—gave us an invitation to tea at the anti-slavery office. 'The ladies too.' 'Was this usual?' 'No, neither were these meetings common; they had not before had their American friends.' We were invited to breakfast the next morning with Elizabeth Pease and parents at their lodgings. Her father was a nice, plain-looking Friend; his wife a thought tastier. We asked Elizabeth about the propriety of going to tea in the evening. 'Go by all means.

'Would she not go?' 'Gladly, if she were invited, but she was not.'"

At five o'clock the delegates repaired to the anti-slavery rooms, large parlors on the second floor. The women were invited to apartments above to disrobe. In the parlors were assembled twenty gentlemen, who received us courteously. Before tea Joseph Sturge said that though this was intended to be a social meeting, and no minutes would be made by the secretary, who had taken our names on entering, yet, that the conversation might be general and confined to anti-slavery topics, he would move William D. Crewdson take the chair. Upon doing so, the latter stated that the committee had requested the company of their American friends that they might have the opportunity of obtaining information respecting the cause which was the interest of all present. He then made an inquiry, to which answers were given by various individuals, each speaking in turn, in conversational style.

"On a table in the room were soon spread slices of bread and butter, and muffins; tea at one end of the table and coffee at the other. The gentlemen officiated, handing the refreshments to guests, who were seated around the room; thus the evening passed delightfully until ten o'clock. To see and hear such men as composed the committee was highly gratifying. Lucretia Mott took part in the conversation, apparently to satisfaction. One of the committee said the company of their women friends had been pleasant. We replied that we should be glad to meet some of our English sisters; the response was, 'You certainly shall.' This was our *début* to the anti-slavery ranks here. Could we have hoped for anything more favorable? Elizabeth Pease called before we separated. We were invited to spend second and fourth day evenings with them in a similar manner."

The committee having charge of the organization of the convention declined to recognize the American women as delegates, admitting them only as spectators. The excluded delegates met and adopted the following protest:

" The American women delegates from Pennsylvania to the World's Convention would present to the committee of the British and Foreign Anti-Slavery Society their acknowledgments for the kind attentions received by them since their arrival in London. But while as individuals they return thanks for these favors, as delegates from the bodies appointing them they deeply regret to learn, by a series of resolutions passed at a meeting of the committee, having reference to credentials from the Massachusetts society, that it is contemplated to exclude women from a seat in the convention as coequals in the advocacy of Universal Liberty. The delegates will duly communicate to their constituents the intimation which these resolutions convey; in the mean time they stand prepared to co-operate to any extent and in any form consistent with their instructions in promoting the just objects of the convention, to which it is presumed will belong the power of determining the validity of any claim to a seat in that body. In behalf of the delegation.

" Very respectfully,

" SARAH PUGH.

" 6th mo. 11th, 1840."

6th mo. 12*th*, 1840.—The convention assembled, the venerable Thomas Clarkson, then in his eighty-first year, presiding. A vote at the first sitting decided that men only were intended to be summoned by the committee which called the convention. Women, however, were admitted as visitors, and assigned seats in an inclosed space on the floor of the hall. A considerable number attended besides the Americans; the latter received much attention and kindness in private.

A protest against the exclusion of the women delegates was read by Wendell Phillips on the last day of the convention, signed by Wendell Phillips, William Adam, Jonathan T. Miller, James Mott, Charles Edwards Lester, George Bradburn, and Isaac Winslow.

Writing to home friends after the meetings, Sarah Pugh says: "Of the convention you will have varying accounts according to the newspapers you may see. One of our friends asked us the other day if we had seen the 'John Bull,' in which we were finely used up; adding, however, that it ridiculed everything that was good. The convention took firm anti-slavery ground, and we all feel satisfied with what it has done in that respect. The manner in which some of the business was conducted, and the strong sectarian feeling evinced by some of its members, particularly the aristocratic Quakers, did not please *us*. It was vexatious to see them so captious on some points that clashed with their orthodoxy while Dr. Bowring and other Unitarians spoke, and also jealous of Lucretia Mott's influence, though she was beyond the bar; yet they could not avoid talking to us and apologizing, complimenting or deprecating our remarks. The poor rejected delegates have been anything but the despised. The women there, with but few exceptions, were not prepared to take our position, though they thanked us most heartily for coming; they would not have been admitted even as visitors had we not come,—now, they say, this privilege will not again be withheld, and they consider it a step gained.

"Our next experience was a gratifying visit to Borough Road School, the original institution founded by Joseph Lancaster, who, while engaged in his vocation of basket-making, was excited to pity by the number of poor children frequenting the streets. He put up some tents in his yard, enticed the children into them, and commenced his school on the monitorial plan. Buildings have been subsequently erected in which the school is continued, and this model institution is an honor to Joseph Lancaster and to its present directors.

"From the school we were driven to the neighborhood of the palace, where the queen was holding a levee; a great occasion, occurring two or three times a year. We halted at the corner of the street for an hour, where we gained a fine view of the princely equipages, the splendor of the trappings, coachmen in curled wigs and cocked hats, ladies inside finely dressed, their heads ornamented with white feathers, some beautiful faces eager with hope,—first presentation perhaps,—others sad and listless, and anon a fat old dowager burdened with jewels and finery."

7th mo. 5th.—"Our company was invited to dine at the house of Mr. Ashurst, a noble-minded lawyer, who resided a few miles from London. Our visit was delightful; a beautiful country situation, highly-cultivated grounds, London in the distance, hill and valley between, —the landscape extending for miles; a pleasant day, and above all, society in which you could breathe freely, —a party of twenty, full of good feeling and liberality. They could hear new things stated without being frightened out of their propriety, though it might conflict with their previous habits of thought. My thoroughly republican feelings were never more strongly realized to be true and right, the deference to rank never seemed more paltry. Here we met William and Mary Howitt and their daughter, a bright girl of sixteen."

7th mo., 1840.—Sarah Pugh and her cousin Abby made a flying visit to Paris, leaving London by rail to Southampton, and steamer thence to Havre. "Our plan was to take the steamer up the Seine, but all the party voted for the diligence,—we so dreaded the water. After sixteen hours' continuous riding through *la belle France*, we arrived in Paris. I shall not attempt a description of its magnificence and its splendors, its old forlorn houses and its narrow streets. Our hotel was near the Tuileries, to the gardens of which we soon repaired. The Place de la Concorde, associated with the most terrific scenes of the Revolution, now magnificent with fountains and statues, beyond the Champs Elysées, the Arch of Triumph terminating the vista, nearly two miles distant,—all, as we stood on the steps of the palace, more than realized my highest imaginations of terrestrial beauty. Ten days were spent, and we had *glanced* at thousands of objects,—to *look* would require months,—but these glances have left images in our minds not to be erased, and well worth the exertion made to obtain them."

7th mo. 26th, 1840.—Sarah and Abby visited Scotland, by way of Matlock and Sheffield; called on James Montgomery, the poet, peeped at Newstead Abbey, York, etc., and passed a few days in George Thompson's home. He accompanied them to Edinburgh. " With Edinburgh we were charmed. The town itself, in its picturesque variety of hill and valley, castle and crags, is inexhaustible in interest,—the more you look the more beautiful it becomes. Here we were joined by James and Lucretia Mott, and proceeded in company to visit Melrose and Dryburgh Abbey and Abbotsford; thence to Tynemouth to see Harriet Martineau, who was suffering with what was thought to be a fatal disease; thence by way of Carlisle, Kendal, and Liverpool to Dublin, where a few days were spent in the home of Richard D. Webb, a convention acquaintance.

" How we breakfasted with one family, dined with another, took tea with a third, rode to Dorkey and Kingston, around the park and the city, walked in filthy lanes and· peeped into miserable hovels, gazed from the top of St. Patrick's Cathedral and at Dean Swift's and Stella's monuments, the house where Mrs. Hemans died, and another in which Daniel O'Connell lives, will not all these be told on our return to America? The plan of breakfast visiting was delightful. At five o'clock A.M. two large jaunting-cars were at the door, the drollest of carriages, the company collected and seated in them, and a refreshing ride of several miles brought us to a stately mansion, where everything was in readiness to entertain a large social breakfast-party. We bade adieu to our Dublin friends and returned to England.

"Passing through the country in this manner we had little opportunity to see the misery that existed in the poverty-stricken districts."

CHAPTER IV.

RETURN TO AMERICA.

On the 26th the party sailed from Liverpool in the packet-ship "Patrick Henry," and after a passage of twenty-nine days arrived in New York. Returning to Philadelphia, Sarah Pugh entered upon a new phase of life. Her school was resigned to others, and her care was chiefly for the comfort of her mother, who was now advanced in years. In the early autumn of 1841 she accompanied Lucretia Mott to Boston to attend a non-resistance meeting, "at which," she writes, "were many of our good folks whom we knew, and we were introduced to many others whom we had known long by name. The meetings were larger than was anticipated, —some three or four hundred. There was an excellent annual report, written and read by Garrison, and much interesting discussion.

"How much are we the creatures of custom! Little faith as I have in drab cloth and broad brims, it seemed strange to me to hear grave and solemn truths uttered by one in the world's garb. *Our* anti-slavery people are mostly Friends, but here was a large body of people zealous and earnest for the right, dressed as the

worldly dress. It is cheering to see great principles
unconnected with sect. During the two days' meetings
we met, at friends' houses, Edmund Quincy, S. J. May,
Adin Ballou, C. H. Whipple, author of that tract on
the evils of the Revolutionary war, and others.

"Maria W. Chapman was a constant study to me.
She is not a talker, but has always the look of deep
thought, though alive to what is passing,—can smile at
a witticism or add a sage remark to serious conversation.
It appears to be her aim *to know the right* and to do it,
to be in everything truthful. Harriet Martineau, in a
letter to a friend, says, 'I cannot but most reverently
regard her spiritual discernment, and the heroism which
is the necessary consequence of it. She acts upon me
with ever-increasing power.'

"At Lynn I met Frederick Douglass. He is about
twenty-four years of age; has been living in New
Bedford for three years,—a good-looking, intelligent,
thoughtful man. Efforts are being made to secure
his freedom; should they be successful he will make
a good agent."

5*th* mo. 21*st*, 1843.—"Many of the tried and true
attended the annual meeting of the American Anti-
Slavery Society, which was cheering to the friends of
freedom. The ready spirit of co-operation was delightful. Extremes met in cordial fellowship, or rather it
was found that extremes were not far apart, and that
there was a oneness of spirit that harmonized all op-
posing elements.

"David Lee Child was appointed editor of the 'Anti-
Slavery Standard.' For myself, I shall not be sorry
if the character of the paper be somewhat different.

Is this flat heresy? I cannot help it. To me it has been a delightful paper, but for some time past it has been a question, Has it not been too delightful? One has always felt comfortable after reading it. It has not incited to action, and roused the spirit nobly to dare and to suffer.

" I feel that we have been content to plod on in a humdrum way, sacrificing little in our love for the quiet and the comfortable. That the cause is making rapid strides I do not doubt, but not by our agency; and though I agree with thee, that 'the process of reason is more convincing than the ranting of fanatical ardor,' yet, may not some of us need the spirit-stirring tones of the enthusiast to rouse our slumbering reason? It may be from the liking of opposites that my lethargic temper is so pleased with the go-ahead energy of our Eastern friends.

"We look forward with great interest to the December meeting. The New England people entered warmly into the idea, and will certainly be here, so we may anticipate a great gathering of the good and true. If *we* are not much benefited I shall be sadly disappointed.

"The 'Universal Inquiry' meetings came after the Anti-Slavery, and were interesting as exhibitions of the upward strivings of the spirit. These queryings may not result in action in our day; but that they will be productive of good I have not a doubt. There are earnest hearts engaged in working out the problem of human happiness for society at large; selfishness is excluded from their theory, and, as far as one may judge, appears not to have a strong hold on the inquirers.

" I remained in New York to attend a religious meeting of a society for Christian Union and Progress; a kind of half-Quaker, half-Unitarian organization. It is certainly in its present state in advance of the sects of the day."

10*th mo.* 6*th*, 1843.—"One of my earliest birthday notes bears record of uneasiness and discomfort at the difference in the outward conditions of those around me. 'Poor old Adam,' the wood-sawyer's, situation is contrasted with my own comparatively luxurious one, and my enjoyment embittered by the contemplation of his harder lot. Now, on this my forty-third birthday, the inequalities of condition is the problem which most interests and perplexes me. Respecting my religious views, the retrospect is painful. How slowly have I worked myself out of the trammels of superstition with which early education had bound me! How long I have been enveloped in fogs, and yet how my soul thirsteth for a knowledge not yet attained!"

1*st mo.* 17*th*, 1844.—" I send you the first number of a periodical edited by William Henry Channing, a man full of faith, hope, and charity; you cannot fail to be charmed by his spirit, if you do not unite with his views. The evils that are in the world, as portrayed by Carlyle's pen of fire, are too painful to contemplate without the hope held out by such bright, cheerful views as Channing presents."

8*th mo.* 4*th*, 1844.—"' No union with slaveholders' is to me a simple, plain doctrine, as is free produce. In my attempt not to partake of the gain of oppression I have not for a moment supposed myself clear; all that I have supposed possible is to cease from *direct* support. If all were to do this, would not the slave be a slave no longer? In respect to the government, cease from all *direct* support of it, and it ceases to be the instrument of bondage. There are two classes who shrink from this simple application of the principle : one, of persons who have determined not to yield their glorious right of sharing in this government, wicked as it is, and therefore look abroad for arguments to justify them in their course; another, who are perhaps morbidly conscientious, who fear to adopt a principle lest, if they fail to carry it out, they convict themselves of sin ; both these classes run into extremes for arguments, and with motives so different use the same plea.

" The article in the last ' Standard,' stating that the principle of ' come-outism' is to withdraw from all political, religious, or *social* connection with wrong-doers, is not true. Political and religious connection implies union in conventional arrangements to support certain principles and measures. Social intercourse is a different thing. It is a part of our nature not to be *come out from* without violating the constitution of our being. Pray not to be taken out of the world, but to be preserved from the evil that is in the world. Between an active supporter of the evil and a passive recipient the difference is so great, it is strange to me that it is not obvious to every mind. . . . In these few words I have attempted to give my idea on separation from iniquity. I do not see in it a Voltaire movement, and even if it were, that *had* its uses, and was *a work to be done*, perhaps not with his spirit. Active benevolence among evil-doers does not require us to support their iniquity. I go into a tavern and mingle with its inmates, but I need not buy a glass of rum to help in its support."

10th mo. 6th, 1844.—"It is now more than two years since I became the care-taker of age, a very different occupation from my former one, less responsible, and not so calculated to call forth the powers of my being. Thanks to the anti-slavery cause, which for the past twelve years has been to me an increasingly absorbing interest, what powers I have may be used, I trust, to some profitable result. Truly, this interest has been and continues to be the blessing of my life. If he who enslaves another fetters himself, may it not be as truly said, he who strives to break the chains of another loosens his own? Courage!"

1st mo., 1846.—"This past week abolitionists of all classes have been rejoicing in the presence of Cassius M. Clay. As a public speaker we must confess to some disappointment; as —— says, 'The truth is we abolitionists have been spoiled by our dainty fare.' Emerson says, 'Eloquence is dog-cheap at the anti-slavery chapel;' and what is good fare for common appetites is poor picking for us, who have so often listened to Garrison, Phillips, and others. Clay's calm, determined expression bespeaks much power.

"First-day morning he was at Cherry Street meeting. Lucretia Mott gave one of her ablest sermons, upon the 'righteousness that exalteth a nation,' and the blessings attendant upon him who giveth even a cup of cold water. In the evening, at Edward M. Davis's tea-table, there was much conversation on moral and physical force, such as would give food for thought to 'the *best shot in Kentucky.*' Verily, abolition makes *extremes* meet, and good is done by this mingling of opposites, this amalgamation. There is everything but success to encourage us, and that will come in good time if we faint not. Success! yes, we have that too. Has not this man been aroused, and will he not awaken others to a sense of their danger and their duty? and then the work will be done. Think of Giddings's speech in Congress! Surely the listeners' ears must have tingled! Look at England; what is agitation doing for her? I rejoice in all this."

10*th mo.* 6*th*, 1846.—"No anniversary record for the past three years. As on the day of the last record, have I looked over those made before, and on reading the closing one, the first prompting was merely to date it again, so precisely does it express my present state. The problems of my being are to me unsolved. At the age of forty-six how sadly can I say, 'My soul waiteth for the Lord'! I long for brighter, clearer, inward manifestations of his presence, a realization of truth, love, beauty, and power in the concrete.

"Not peace, not happiness, not assurance, but *childlike* submission, childlike faith, and meek-eyed blessedness."

5*th mo.* 19*th*, 1848.—"The long-hoped-for Wendell Phillips unexpectedly made his advent among us for a few days. His speeches were elegant, lucid, and powerful. I thought even determined opponents must be convinced that his positions were correct, and if conscientious, they must henceforth sustain them. The charm of his oratory was great.

"Another light has arisen upon us, William Henry Channing. The 'Associationists' dedicated their hall, and he was one of the 'ministering angels' on the occasion. His sermon at Furness's church was a beautiful display of goodness, imagination, and veneration."

5th mo. 26th, 1850. (To a friend who had recently visited Washington.)—"Are we not thankful that this struggle is going on in our country,—now no longer apathetic,—and that we can witness it, and are in a degree capable of appreciating the importance of the contest? The blessing is now as in former times on the eyes that see and the ears that hear the things that make for true peace and salvation. . . . To look at the idols which this nation has set up, and to judge by the outward manifestations the interior worth, is interesting, and places in the mind's gallery pictures instead of ideals. How differently do I now regard the originals of those placed in my mind in the spring of '34! What a flaming Whig partisan was I then,—full of the glory of Webster, Clay, and Preston! Surely I am not mistaken in believing that I now look on these men with 'anointed eyes,' and my present regard for them is much nearer the true standard of their worth. How truly 'Ichabod' is written upon it! Blessings on Whittier for his expression of the feeling of all true hearts, and blessings on him, too, for his kind, good letter to Garrison, and blessings on Furness for his full expression of the thoughts that glowed within him. It was my happiness to be at New York a witness of the scenes of that day that Furness pronounces 'the greatest of his life.' It was indeed a joy to witness his 'transfiguration,' inspired as he was by the spirit of the hour; to see the orator of the pulpit transformed into the orator of the forum, the man of the desk into

4

the man of that free platform, the air of which he breathed as his native element.   Its invigorating power does not pass away with the excitement of the moment; it inspires his pulpit services and his daily converse; he talks of it by the wayside and by the fireside."

8*th mo.* 11*th*, 1850.—"And you are interested in the knockings and rappings.   I am curious to know the result of C.'s investigations.   Manifestations so clumsy do not take my fancy.   A still, small voice is much more consonant to my ideas of the spirit language."

10*th mo.* 6*th*, 1850.—" My fiftieth birthday!   Almost a life, and how spent?   What am I?   Where am I?   What must be the record?   My life as a whole has been aimless, objectless.   Not that I would account this to myself as criminal: only state it as a fact that not to any important work has my life been devoted; therefore no result is visible of efforts made, of aims accomplished.   That each day has had its round of small duties, and that these have been performed to some extent to the best of my abilities.   This, at least, I have outgrown, an ascetic condemnation of myself. Neither would I glory, for what have I to boast?   This comprises my outward life.   Of the internal, what can be said?   That, after years of continued fruitless and unprofitable questionings that would not be laid, a 'childlike submission,' a 'childlike faith' has sprung up in my heart, small as a grain of mustard-seed; yet, I trust, destined to grow into an ever-present feeling. 'He doeth all things well.'"

12*th mo.* 25*th*, 1850. (Referring to the death of Mary Agnew Taylor.)—" One sad subject is prominent, —the final departure from among you of what was once so beautiful, so fair, and to you who knew her well a treasure of such worth that to lose it is grief unutterable. Again comes the question 'What is life, and to what does it tend?'"

1*st mo.* 12*th*, 1851.—"In early life what 'the world' was, puzzled me greatly. As expounded from the Friends' gallery it was, to my simple mind, every one that dressed 'gay.' Its spirit has been too manifest in these latter days for me to be ignorant of it now."

3*d mo.* 3*d*, 1851.—"Last evening Lucretia Mott spoke on Woman's Rights before a society called by the world infidels, by themselves 'Friends of Progress,' who meet weekly for improvement, inviting addresses on the important questions of the day. An intelligent audience listened with attention and apparent interest to the exposition of the subject. It was comforting to see so many willing to entertain the question.

"Alas for Fredrika Bremer! We had hoped more from her. Her vision ought not to be obscured by the clouds that have gathered round those brought up under the influence of this monster curse of slavery. I do not wonder that colonization commends itself to just such minds and hearts as hers, for if ever Satan was clothed as an angel of light, deceiving the benevolent, it is in this scheme."

4*th mo.* 18*th*, 1851.—"I have been reading with great interest the 'Life of Andrew Combe,' written by his brother George. The interest in part was in seeing how care and skill were able to ward off the final effects of disease, and to enable him to live a comfortable, useful, and happy life. I was not aware, till reading this book, how little attention has been paid by the medical faculty to the science of *preserving* health, and how much has been done for humanity by Dr. Combe's works on Physiology. My faith increases, if possible, in the benefits of fresh air and exercise as preservatives and restoratives ; though, like all other good things, they *may* be used to excess."

In the spring of 1851, Sarah Pugh's mother received an injury by a fall in her room, which confined her to bed, and, after four months of suffering, she died on the 28th of Eighth month. To the devoted daughter this loss of the central object of her love and care appeared for a time almost overpowering. Her usual duties were performed with her accustomed equanimity, but the main-spring of effort seemed broken.

10*th mo. 6th,* 1851.— " My fifty-first birthday. 'Since the last, solemn reign of this day of reflection' on the 28th of Eighth month, after an illness of four months, the one who, above all others, loved me, *my Mother !* has passed away from me, and her place here shall know her no more forever. What to me will be my future life without this central point of love and devotion? There are objects of interest and importance abounding on all sides, but what faculties, what powers, have I to effect anything in connection with them ? May what there is of ability in me be so employed as to obtain the reward, above all others, ' Well done, good and faithful servant' !"

CHAPTER V.

SECOND VISIT TO EUROPE.

IN the autumn, deciding to join her brother and sister-in-law, who were travelling in Europe, she sailed for Havre, landing at that port on the 28th of Eleventh month, and reached Paris two days before the famous *coup d'état* of Louis Napoleon.

12*th mo.* 2*d*, 1851.—" Glancing through the window about ten o'clock, we observed crowds of people hastening towards the Tuileries, companies of soldiers, horse and foot. Much excitement was visible."

12*th mo.* 3*d*, 1851.—" Walked a mile to the English Ambassador's. The streets were as usual; all we met seemed intent on what was before them of business or pleasure. On our return we took a cab and drove to the prefect of police, crossing the Seine by the Tuileries. Here the scene was changed; in the street groups of well-dressed men and women stopping to read the proclamations which are posted up in every direction; soldiers at different points. Alighting at the office, we found all the courts and places around filled with troops. The sentinel challenged us, but at the word ' passport' allowed us to proceed, as we did, passing between companies of soldiers and their stacked guns; six or eight companies, of twenty or more each, were grouped round fires of wood built on the pavement, many with huge loaves of bread tied on their knapsacks.

"On the 7th, at eight o'clock, we walked on the Boulevard. It seemed difficult to realize that this splendid avenue, with its long lines of brilliant lamps, crowded with gay equipages as well as pedestrians, and its shops filled with the works of artistic skill, had so lately been the scene of destruction and death. Each one was now resuming his usual habits and occupations,— what else could be done?—but there was no levity; most countenances were serious, many sad, all anxious.

"From Paris we went on the 15th by rail to Chalons, and took boat on the 16th for Lyons. Fog on the river stopped the boat, and we were taken by diligence to Avignon, by rail to Marseilles, and steamer to Leghorn, where my brother and sister met me. The boat stopped at Leghorn for the day, which gave opportunity to see Pisa, and the voyage was then continued to Civita Vecchia, whence six hours by diligence took us to Rome, where we arrived on Christmas eve.

"The next morning we witnessed high mass at St. Peter's. The contrast between the manger cradle with its attending shepherds and the magnificence before me, the song of Peace on earth and good-will to men with the swords and halberds of the Swiss guards and French soldiers, was constantly in my mind. The Swiss guards in their parti-colored dress, stripes of buff, red, and black, a most harlequin garb, and the long lines of soldiers that raised and lowered their swords in response to various parts of the ceremony, made more intense the feelings of the hour.

"We spent several weeks in Rome, obtaining quiet

apartments, and on the morning of New-Year's day, 1852, I sallied forth, going to the Piazza del Popolo, where the Corso, the Chestnut Street or Broadway of Rome, commences, then through the Corso its whole length to the Capitoline Hill. The shops, save confectioners', were shut, the people out in their holiday dress,—except for the soldiers, priests in canonicals of various colors, and a few peasants, you might suppose yourself in America. I threaded my way through places which I wished to see; I am satisfied to have seen them,—never wish to see them again, any more than I would make for pleasure a second visit to Baker Street. The houses of the people and the streets were wretched and dirty, but the sun shone warm, and the comparatively well-dressed men, women, and children were basking in its rays. A little farther on was the Piazza del Consolation, and the Coliseum, through which I wandered, meeting only French soldiers, the guards of the place, and a procession of priests clothed in white, chanting in their peculiar strain. The ruins, the soldiers, the priests, the shrines, encompassed with a delicious air and canopied by a clear blue sky,—was not this glory enough for one day?

" On the evening of the 6th the moon was full, the night clear. 'Now for the Coliseum!' and away our party went. It was a glorious sight,—the moon in the meridian, the stars in the far-off heavens, and the wondrous pile around us, more wonderful than it seems possible to conceive. Preceded by a guide we ascended from one platform to another, each view more beautiful than the last; then by the light of a blazing torch descended through the dark passages, catching occasional

glimpses of the moonlight through the broken arches,
—a picture in the mind's gallery not to be displaced.
Returning, we drove to a fair held the night before
Epiphany, which is here what Christmas is to us. It
was in the open street, occupying a square or more with
booths. The toys, etc., were of the most common kind,
as this is for 'the people,' and an amusing scene it was,
something like a little carnival. All was orderly and
peaceful, the chief noise being of children's whistles,
which were blown continually. Thus we made one step
from the sublime, if not to the ridiculous, at least to the
funny. Next day, Epiphany, we visited a church near
the Capitol, where a large doll, dressed as an infant
Jesus, was carried in procession round the church and
held up to the view of the hundreds outside, that their
children, if sick, might be healed !

"My great interest was the sight of the people, who
thronged the church and the broad flight of one hundred steps leading to it; they were 'the people' and
the peasantry from the neighboring districts, who, in
varied picturesque and deplorable costume, crowded to
witness this, their special ceremony. The more I see
of what is around me the more I feel that I know
nothing of their life, that my thoughts are not their
thoughts. This sense of ignorance, if it were only the
first step to knowledge, might be the more patiently
borne. I did not see much of the beggars of Rome.
There are some forlorn objects, that you always see if
you walk in certain directions; such objects as would
be shut from sight in our almshouses at home, who
here bask in the warm sun and excite the sympathy
of the many strangers who frequent these places. I

have walked hours in the worst parts of the city and
not seen a beggar ; on the contrary, the artisan has
been busy at his trade, and the women sewing or knitting at their open doors,—windows this class rarely
have,—their abodes are in the lowest stories of high
houses in narrow streets.   Imagine a row of houses
four or five stories high, the upper stories brightened
by the sun ; in the basement, on a level with the street,
rooms about fifteen feet square,—one may be a carpenter's shop, the next a green-grocer's, the third a stable,
the fourth a baker's,—all with rough, large wooden
shutters or doors, that are taken down in the daytime
to admit light and air.   On the Corso are the most
elegantly-arranged dry-goods stores, and between them
and those first mentioned ranges, in every variety, the
trade of Rome.

" At first the people struck me as homely, but, now
that I know them better, I am often charmed with
their fine faces, particularly their hair, forehead, and
eyes ; the lower· part of the face is not so good.   I
must not forget one part of the exhibition of the Bam-
bino festival.   The church was crowded long before
the priests commenced their performance.   To instruct
and interest the assembled host, who are not seated but
walking through the immense church, a boy, some eight
years old, was mounted on a platform to address the
people, which he did apparently with great effect; they
gathered round him, listening to his fervent speech and
impassioned gestures for full fifteen minutes ; then, in
succession, two little girls (what an argument for the
woman question !) held the delighted hundreds in rapt
attention."

1st mo. 23*d*, 1852.—" As housekeeper I have had some experience in the domestic line. My shopping is quite ludicrous. Once, wanting some brown sugar, after having said 'zucchero,' held up my fingers for the number of pounds, and had the white weighed in a sheet of heavy paper laid in the scales, I puzzled my brain to think how I should tell I wanted brown also, for it was not in sight. Luckily, the man had on a coat precisely the color; to this I pointed, said 'zucchero,' held up my hand, and my want was supplied. Our housekeeping is a simple affair. Bread, muffins, milk, and butter are brought to us every morning. The maid makes the fire, sets the tea-kettle before it, cleans the parlor, and lays the table for breakfast before we enter the room.

" After breakfast, there is no more care for the day, unless we make an extempore lunch of bread and stewed fruit, prunes or apples; stewing this fruit or boiling milk to pour over bread is the amount of our cooking. We do this that we may have more food that is not meat; so much of what is sent from the ' trattoria' for our dinner is flesh; always soup and two or three kinds of meat and one vegetable; and, though we charge them again and again *always* to send potatoes, they may not come three times a week.

" Home papers were received at Naples containing a report of the Woman's Rights Convention at Worcester; seating myself in full view of the charming scenery before us, to which my eyes were often raised, I enjoyed communion with Wendell Phillips, Abby K. Foster, and W. H. Channing. Amid the grandeur and beauty that surrounded me came the feeling, there is

something beyond all these in the *moral* world and the
ability to appreciate its greatness. Such, too, was the
feeling in Rome, surrounded by the works of high art ;
though with a deep sense of my ignorance, I covet
greatly the knowledge rightly to appreciate the beauty
and power of the arts by which so many great and noble
minds have given to the world their ideas of the good
and the true."

2d mo. 8th.—" The tomb of Virgil is in a wild, beautiful ravine overlooking the city; our ascent to it was
through innumerable lines of washed linen, as if all
Naples was hung up to dry, and such a display of rags
and patches it would be difficult for you to imagine.
Indeed, from the clothing of thousands of the people,
you would suppose that never in their lives had they
known the luxury of a new garment; patch upon patch
makes up the whole dress. At whatever beautiful place
you stop you are surrounded by a troop of ill-dressed
peasants, and, excepting in cases of weakness from disease or age, they appear a hardy, well-fed race, the children pretty, black-eyed, fat, and rosy. Their incessant
importunity is a sad drawback upon your enjoyment,—
one of the many taxes of sight-seeing, which, pleasant
as it is in memory, has its price at the time. In Italy, as
in Rome, I see a large industrious population, in many
cases not enlightened industry certainly, for the distaff
and the hand-saw do the work of the spinning-machine
and saw-mill. It is a continual astonishment to me to
see with how little these poor people content themselves,
and how much would be possible to them were they
permitted by the ruling powers to use the gifts with
which God and nature have endowed them. In the

midst of the lazzaroni districts—for there is no particular one—you see quite an appearance of *doing something*, tending a fruit or shell stall, twirling the distaff,
or rocking the basket cradle. How I covet schools for
the hundreds of children that are basking in the warm
sun, looking as though they would be delighted with
anything that employed their faculties! The happiest-
looking boys we see are those in the shops of the
workmen, and the girls who are sitting at the doors
knitting. *Women stand* at their doors and knit; the
stockings of the people are thus manufactured; many,
however, wear *none*, nor even shoes, though now mid-
winter."

2d mo. 24th.—"Often I quote the old proverb with
variations, 'Travellers meet with strange companions.'
I have just returned from a drive to a splendid villa,
a Jesuit priest one of our carriage-party. His long
black dress and broad-brimmed, looped-up hat made,
as it always does to me, a most incongruous part in
every-day life. To see and hear these priests laugh and
talk, as they can right merrily, excites in me the kind
of surprise a child feels to find kings common men,
and that they sleep without their crowns. We met our
priest at the American Minister's; he could talk some
English, and was anxious to express in that language
his longing to go to America, 'that free country;' here
there was no hope for liberty, 'the cannon were
so strong.' I tried to give the idea that there was
something stronger than cannon, but, though I was
astonished at my own eloquence on the non-resistance
question, I much fear that my words failed to convey
their full import to his mind, especially as Mrs. ——,

of our party, burst forth in patriotic admiration of the
frigate ' Independence,' now lying in the bay, and
which yesterday was decked from stem to stern with
flags in honor of the 22d."

2d mo. 26th, 1852.—" Yesterday we drove to the
Campo Santo, the Laurel Hill of Naples, five miles distant. It is a beautiful spot, far surpassing the famed Père
la Chaise,—the variety of the ground, the view of the
bay, the low country, and Vesuvius, with the profusion
of flowers in summer, for even now the roses, hyacinths,
jonquils, pyrus japonica, and rosemary are in bloom.
You must know the thoughts that crowded upon me in
such a place,—the hallowed spot on our own beautiful
river. The arrangements in this cemetery are of the
best: there is a large room in which the bodies are at
first placed ; cords are put in the hands, attached to
bells, which, if rung, would summon immediate assistance ; a lamp, too, is kept burning at night. The
bodies are deposited in vaults for fifteen months ere
they are buried in the ground. We saw in the street
a carriage for the dead, all yellow and gold, the most
gorgeous and gay of vehicles.

" The trees have a melancholy look at this season, and
are not much brighter in summer. The great want in
the beauty of the country is trees. Except on the roads,
which are bordered with them, you scarcely see one
worthy the name ; even where there is an effort to grow
into a tree, the only result is a slender crooked stem
that has been greatly hindered in its growth,—like the
people, mentally.

" Returning to Rome, we left that city 3d mo. 18th,
by vetturino, for France, visiting Narni, the Falls of

Terni, and Lake Thrasymene. At Florence we met some American friends, and spent an evening with the family of Powers, the sculptor. The conversation was not on the Greek Slave, or any other model of beauty in the outward world, but on the things which pertain to the inward life of man. Powers is a Swedenborgian, much interested in his faith, which has given him peace and joy. We proceeded by rail to Leghorn, and by steamer to Genoa, a strange old town, with its high houses, narrow streets, and bright-shawled women,—large cotton shawls of the brightest-colored flowers and animals,—lions, panthers, etc. Thence by a beautiful ride along the Mediterranean, in sight of snow-clad mountains, we reached Nice and Marseilles, and proceeded to Paris, arriving there 4th mo. 7th, 1852.

"There was little interest in the country through which we passed in France, save in the contrast it presented to that which we had left: low, flat ground in the place of rugged mountains and deep glens, houses with pointed roofs and wooden shutters instead of heavy tiles and iron-barred windows, and, in lieu of a great variety of fanciful head-gear, the women universally were dressed in pretty, neat caps. In place of priests, shrines, and churches we saw newspapers— such as they are—in the houses of a few persons. In Italy we did not see one of the natives reading, unless it might be a prayer-book. Then, too, everything looks new; as much newer than Italy as America looks newer than France.

"I received in Paris a package of two 'Liberators' and 'Liberty Bells,' the former of which I devoured;

after so long an abstinence they were as nectar and ambrosia to me. Such is the 'food convenient for me.' Pictures and statues *gratify*, they do not *satisfy* the cravings of my soul.

"Visits to Versailles and other points, in company with M. W. Chapman and Mrs. Putnam, and a call on the Brownings, occupied several days; on the 15th we left Paris, stopping at Amiens, to see the cathedral and the hall in which the treaty of 1802 was signed, then by rail to Brussels."

4th mo. 18*th*.—"Level, highly-cultivated country; many windmills, peat-bogs, and coal-beds, women and girls wheeling the barrows. There is, however, an air of comfort and cleanliness in the appearance of the poorest houses; instead of the dung-heaps, etc., of Italy, there is the clean-swept yard or well-kept garden. Brussels is a quiet, clean city. Many things here are home-like, —the brightly-polished door-plates,—and yesterday, though quite cold, for the first time we saw window and pavement washing. Of the two extremes, give me this over Italian filth. Strange inconsistency, we are annoyed with the men smoking and spitting.

"On the field of Waterloo we had an extensive view of a finely-cultivated country, from a mound nearly two hundred feet high, raised over the bodies of the slain. Nowhere could the eye rest on a more peaceful scene; quiet hamlets and clusters of houses for miles around. Thirty-seven years have passed since that battle of the nations. Napoleon and his thousands have taken their place in 'the silent halls of death,' Wellington soon will follow them. 'Thus passeth this world away.' Thence to London, *via* Mechlin

and Antwerp, where we spent a day in viewing the
churches and picture-galleries. At Antwerp we found
the finest paintings of Rubens and Vandyke, and the
most elaborately-carved wood in the world. The
works of these painters rose wonderfully in our esti-
mation seen in this their native country, where one
rises so far above the mere portrait-painter, and the
other is not degraded into the flatterer of Marie de
Medicis. The carving in wood almost rivalled the
marble of the Vatican.

"In London we met Mrs. Follen and her sister, George
Thompson, and others, with whom various places of
interest were visited, the British Museum, Zoölogical
and Botanic Gardens, the Houses of Parliament, etc.
Went next morning to the Crystal Palace, which is
beautiful in its naked simplicity, and its huge size beyond my idea. The service at Christ Church, where
were upwards of a thousand of the Blue-coat boys, was
interesting, also the hospital where the boys dine,—so
many healthy, well-behaved children. At Hampton
Court, the grounds pleased me as much as the pictures;
but my especial satisfaction was seeing the cartoons of
Raphael, realizing the wishes of childhood. I met
Louis Blanc at a literary party. He is quite diminu-
tive in stature, interesting in countenance, but as his
animated conversation was entirely in French, I can,
alas! tell nothing more. Professor Newman lectured
before the Italian Society; Mazzini was present, and
made a short address in well-written but badly-spoken
English.

"The 'Pennsylvania Freeman' has been such a treat
to me! Time, space, vanish, and the very atmosphere

of 31 North Fifth Street, with all its loved associations, is around me,—the Committee, the Female Anti-Slavery Society, the Fair Committee, collectively and individually,—once more I am in my old element, with the feeling of a fish *in* water.

"I met by appointment a Miss Evans, translator of Strauss, at present assistant editor of the 'Westminster Review,' and tried to interest her in our anti-slavery movement, as she is a clear thinker, and may have much in her power. At Mrs. Reed's a pleasant and elegant dinner-party of friends and neighbors, that Mrs. Reed wished *me* to interest in our cause. But, alas! the most brilliant one among them has devoted herself to the High Church, believing it all-powerful to save.

"Mrs. Rotch, a venerable lady who had expressed a wish to *see me,* is eighty-eight years of age,—that was to me the great attraction. We found her in her drawing-room, seated erect, in a large rocking-chair sent her from America. She is slightly deaf, and her memory of names not good, otherwise she is bright and alive to what is passing around her, retaining her interest for America and Americans. Speaking of the remarks made on the paucity of their contributions to the Exhibition, I said, 'You must remember that America is young,—that I, a woman now living, remember when we used to ask for *the return of a pin* that had been borrowed, and one of our school mottoes was, "To see a pin and let it lie, you'll come to want before you die."'

"The evening was spent at Mrs. Follen's. George Thompson, Mr. Schoelcher, Miss Evans, and Miss Murray. There was some anti-slavery talk, but the evening was principally occupied with the rappings.

What they call facts *vex me*, they are so wonderful and yet so silly. Mrs. Follen is much interested, and longs for communication with the spirit world, which I confess I do not, if it must be by means of material knockings."

Liverpool, 5th mo. 13th.—"This English domestic scenery is surpassingly lovely ; it may be tame, but for ' mine abode' give it me in preference to the crags that are wild and majestic,—that is, those that I have seen, —taking both with their accompaniments."

CHAPTER VI.

ANTI-SLAVERY WORK ABROAD.

AT the instance of anti-slavery friends in England who believed that Sarah Pugh could do a good work in a private way in that country, she decided to remain when her brother and sister sailed for home, 5th mo. 15th. After their departure she visited Harriet Martineau at her home and Elizabeth Pease at Ben Rhydding water-cure, and then went to Dublin, where in the family of Richard D. Webb she spent several weeks, visiting friends, making occasional excursions, attending some anti-slavery meetings, etc. "An ex-mayor of Cork, at one party, gave some interesting statistics of the improvement of Ireland within the last five years ; some workhouses that had contained two hundred inmates now numbering only twenty. There is

misery and degradation here, certainly, but as certainly
not so much as formerly, and *improvement, here* as in
England, is the order of the day. There is comfort in
this, even though it be slow. When can it be said of
our own country?

" At St. Stephen's Church I saw and heard good Arch-
bishop Whately, a plain-speaking man above sixty,
much like Bishop Potter. Of course he is not popular
with those who think the Church has to do only with
spiritual things; he is, however, loved and reverenced
by the community at large.

" An excursion was made with Richard D. Webb to
County Wicklow; separated from the county of Dublin by a range of mountains. We passed through a
wild gap, the country cultivated and picturesque; saw
three real mountain tarns, overshadowed by dark hills,
and the water colored by bogs, through which the
streamlets flow. The day proved propitious for sight-
seeing, as there was every variety of light and shade,
of sunshine and· showers, to diversify the prospect,—
now all brightness and beauty, anon all darkness and
grandeur, as the sunlight played on the mountains, or
mist and clouds enveloped their summits. Then the
showers gave another variety to the day, in the views
afforded of the life of the people, the shelter in a wayside inn, with its gallery of art, composed of penny
pictures of the saints, interspersed with Red Riding-
Hoods and specimens of chirography; in a cottage of
three rooms, tenanted by three little, rosy-cheeked,
curly-headed children; the parents gone to mass. We
had full leisure and opportunity to inspect the earthen-
floored habitation. The *room* contained a curtained

bed, covered with a white Marseilles counterpane, both ragged, and the canopy of the one covered with dust. A chest of drawers, on the top of which, amidst a variety of trumpery, such as plates, combs, doll's cradles, etc., were several pounds of raw beefsteak and a lump of butter, evident signs of good living.

"Is it not strange how the Irish cling to their national jaunting-car? I tell them that at home it will seem almost incredible that a vehicle without any protection from the weather is the chosen conveyance of a people whose climate does not afford them one hundred clear days in the year, three-fourths of their time their only protection umbrellas and cloaks. 'Oh, they are so cheerful and so airy and so pleasant and so handy, and everything else that is good; and then I can't bear to be shut up in a covered car, they are so close, so stifling.' Thus tastes differ, though I must confess myself half converted.

"For one thing I was not prepared, the low estimate of Americans generally felt here by the classes not the *low;* the latter, judging by their actions, emigrating to us when they can, think differently. Of course, to me they are polite, and try to avoid anything that would lead me to suppose they had not an exalted opinion of the country; but it is this effort that makes it evident the feeling exists; America is large and grand, but the Americans are uncultivated.

"Yesterday, the Lord Lieutenant, his lady, and ourselves, with about a thousand others of the nobility and gentry of Dublin, visited an exhibition of the Royal Irish Horticultural Society. It was held in beautiful grounds at Monktown,—flowers arranged in four marquees. Some of the flowers were beautiful, but the great beauty and attraction to me were the human flowers. So far as my opportunity of observation has extended, the Irish are a more refined people than the English, more of elegance and grace in their bearing. The common people have more of the humanities in their composition. My heart warms to this people. When I am domiciled with the English, *they* may be in the ascendant.

"Richard D. Webb and myself went on an excursion to Ballitore, the seat of the school conducted by Abraham Shackleton and his son Richard, in which Edmund Burke was a pupil. A descendant lives in a large house near the village, surrounded by finely-cultivated grounds, flowers, fruit, shrubs, and trees, all of which are his wife's especial care and delight. The grounds here owe much to the cheapness of labor, a man being hired for twenty cents a day. Our host has a farm of two hundred acres, about sixty of it farmed, the rest pasture and plantations ; on these he generally employs fifteen men, sometimes twenty or thirty."

7th mo. 17*th.*—"I must tell you of our visit to the venerable Mr. and Mrs. Hutton. On our arrival at the two-hundred-year-old house, a mile from the city, we were met by Mrs. Hutton. 'Would we walk in the garden before we unshawled?' She accompanied us, pointing out this beautiful flower and that fine shrub ; leading us to one particular bush, among many fine ones the finest, 'This I call Lucretia Mott;' and surely such a bush and such gooseberries mortal eyes do not often behold. In the drawing-room we were received by Mr. Hutton, eighty-seven years old, somewhat feeble. A daughter about fifty and two grand-sons, eight and ten, compose the family. Sons and their wives, grandchildren and cousins, increased the party to about twenty. Among all these, Mr. and Mrs. Hutton were the bright particular stars; Mrs. Hutton in her eighty-sixth year, an erect form, a smiling face, *flaxen* hair, *not gray*, fair complexion; then the sensible remark, the varied expression, the lively interest in the things that pertained to progress and improvement, betokened a mind fully alive to the great questions of the day. Reviews, Travels, and 'Uncle Tom's Cabin' were familiar.

" Mr. Lupton, an English gentleman, speaking of the Fugitive Slave Law, which is incomprehensible here, said that when he first heard of it he would not believe it; it was impossible such a law could be passed; that it was a fiction of the ultra-abolitionists. Now he says he cannot imagine any honorable or honest man could retain an office which would oblige him to act under it, for the law itself offers a *bribe*."

A distinguished surgeon of Bristol, England, Mr. Estlin, with his daughter, active anti-slavery laborers, arrived in Dublin, and shortly afterwards Sarah Pugh accompanied them to Cork.

The day following, " a friend called in her jaunting-car and drove us to see the environs, which are beautiful; high hills, cultivated and adorned with houses and trees. In one of these, surrounded by a lawn, the greenness of which was exquisite, lived the brother of Father Mathew, who generally spent his First-days there. We were fortunate in meeting Father Mathew. He greeted us cordially, spoke of 'beautiful Philadelphia.' He is in appearance much like his pictures. As we drove through the lawn we met a company of three returning from taking the pledge; during the half-hour we remained several more came, and before we left we accompanied him to the hall, and saw him administer the pledge to eight persons, five women and three children. They were a reverential group. More were coming, and his brother's wife, a charming woman, who, with her family, 'dotes' on Father Mathew, said it was thus all day; that he left his dinner three times that day to administer the pledge, preferring not to keep them waiting."

7th mo. 26th, 1852.—"One of Father Mathew's converts of twenty years' standing, a thriving tradesman in a small way, has lately become much interested in anti-slavery, and that he may *do* something has commenced the manufacture of free ginghams, which he sells as low as slave-labor produce. He employs nineteen looms."

7th mo. 27th.—"This morning was spent in the Exhibition, which is quite a creditable affair, and as it is entirely composed of Irish productions, was the more interesting. The poplin, of course, is unequalled elsewhere, and is rich and beautiful beyond any I ever saw; the lace and knitting wonderful; both these the work of the peasantry. One part of the building was a gallery of fine arts; some pictures by Maclise, of Cork, said, I know not how truly, to be among the greatest of modern painters."

After an excursion to Killarney, Sarah Pugh with the Estlins proceeded to Bristol, where she was soon at home with her valued friends.

9th mo. 12th.—"The most ridiculous things I see in

this country are the dresses of the liveried servants and the charity schools : little boys in blue breeches and bright-red or yellow stockings, and girls—I saw a hundred passing the other day—in red frocks, white aprons, capes, and long knit gloves,—the Red Maids' School. There are other charity schools of which the dress is not so conspicuous, though a uniform. Bristol abounds in charitable associations, many of them commenced by the Unitarians, and continued with assistance from others. I have been reading accounts of them with much interest. A number of original letters of Mr. and Mrs. Barbauld, Dr. Priestley, Southey, and Coleridge were shown me, written to Mr. Estlin's father, a Unitarian of this place, and a journal kept by his wife of a tour to Paris in 1789; the details of the difficulties of their journey were such a contrast to the present facilities for accomplishing the same; the description of the *boorish* peasants and the splendor of church processions, etc. Then their arrival in Paris, and the interest of the period; a few days after their arrival the Revolution broke out, and the Bastile was demolished! The incidents and feelings of the times were described with a glowing pen, with great sympathy for the people, and ardent hopes for the future. It seemed like reading of the Revolution in '48, so similar the moderation and nobility in both cases, alas! how repaid! I also read some letters of Rammohun Roy, and an account of his funeral solemnities. He was buried in the grounds of the lady at whose house he died, a few miles from this place. Mr. Estlin was his physician, and they were intimate friends; all speak of him with great interest and affection."

9th mo. 17th.—" Went to Bath to meet a committee of the Ladies' Anti-Slavery Society; a pleasant conference with some dozen persons, and I was happy to give explanations on points which had embarrassed their movements.

" William Blair, who was the chairman of the convention in 1840, after Clarkson retired, came to breakfast. We went together over parts of the anti-slavery action since '40, and I trust I was able to disabuse his mind of some unfounded prejudices against Garrison.

" Walking around the town, I stopped at the Hot Baths. The water is an unpleasant greenish color, not clear, as it comes up into the main public bath, some thirty feet square, at the rate of three hogsheads a minute; temperature 116°. Home by moonlight, but not *such* moonlight as ours. Occasionally, for some hours in the day, the skies may look as intensely and beautifully blue as our own, so that the inhabitants of these islands may have some idea of what ours are; but no evening splendor that I have seen will compare with ours. First-day, at eleven o'clock, we went to Friends' meeting,—the house once a Catholic chapel. There are but few Friends here; two men in the gallery, no preacher. Friends' burying-ground joins our friends' grounds; a small square plot planted with trees and shrubbery, the ground level and sodded; the place of a grave marked by a small square stone with name and age on it, placed there by the Monthly Meeting."

Bristol, 9th mo. 21st.—" We called at the ' Red Lodge,' so styled from the color of the outside of the house. The large drawing-room is wainscoted with richly-carved and polished oak, now as black as ebony.

6

The room would be dark but for the large windows which make one side almost entirely glass from a lofty ceiling to the floor. In this room Queen Elizabeth breakfasted on one of her journeys. The room was worthy of royalty,—if royalty was worthy of it.

"The Duke is gathered to his fathers; of course, you see some of the high-wrought eulogiums with which the press is rife. I was interested the other day at the railway station to see the book-stall had placards, 'Life of Wellington,' on one side 'Uncle Tom,' and on the other 'The White Slave.' There are now four editions of 'Uncle Tom,' one as low as sixpence. Literature here is becoming cheap and accessible to the multitude, and efforts are made, in all ways save national, to teach the people. We may hope that the rising generation will not be so ignorant as some now on the stage. A farmer of Somersetshire, on hearing parts of 'Uncle Tom' read, said he did not know there were any slaves now in the world.

"A twelve miles' ride to Clevedon, in Somersetshire, on the Bristol Channel, by rail through a highly-cultivated country, one of the apple- and cider-making counties. The orchards were the finest I have seen here; they do not compare with those of America. Fruit and vegetables are not, as with us, staples : more meat, bread, and cheese; the rich eat more meat than with us, the poor more bread; fruit is a luxury, though just now pears and plums are rather cheap, ten or a dozen of each sold for a penny. You may judge by their selling by number that they are not abundant. Occasional presents are sent from the neighboring gentry who grow wall fruit; the nectarines taste like

our peaches, the peaches poor. At Clevedon we walked
on the shore and clambered up hills; the views from
these exceedingly fine. Parts of our ramble led us by
farm-houses and over roads resembling *American;* the
square, upright, snug house, with some attempt at
flowers and shrubbery, yet evidently showing these
were not the main consideration."

10*th mo.* 3*d.*—"We had an anti-slavery committee
and a few friends invited to meet them; twenty-five
earnest souls, desirous to do something for the poor
slave. Some were anxious for means to do without the
produce of the slave's toil, and all wished to be enlightened on the workings of the system as it affected religious bodies in America, on the negro pew, on the
separate seats in Friends' meetings; was it really true
they were seated on one side?"

10*th mo.* 6*th.*—"My birthday, spent quietly in this
English home, with the feeling that I was far away
from those who might feel interested in the event. Of
course, the many varied scenes of the past year came
before me with grateful remembrance, accompanied
with the feeling which is so often with me, how little
we know of the future. Not that I would have it
otherwise; what is right to do for the present is the
great thing, when the choice is apparently in our own
hands.

"Took tea at Mr. A.'s, a Unitarian minister. He
had a long letter from a young friend, an Englishman,
travelling in America. It was sorrowful to see the
apologies and excuses he made for slavery. It seems
to me that instead of England helping America on
this subject, there is great fear that American influences

will depress the tone of anti-slavery feeling in this country; therefore it is especially necessary for those who see the right faithfully to maintain it."

10*th mo.* 12*th.*—"On First-day went to Friends' meeting, after which I was taken to see the school-rooms connected with the meeting-house. The house was formerly a Catholic chapel; the schools were in the parts that had been a monastery, the cloisters now the play-house. When Friends got possession of the property, called 'The Friars,' the buildings were in a dilapidated condition; built in 1200; they are now restored much in harmony with the original plan, and, in furnishing, the oldest of black-oak desks and chairs were procured, to be in keeping with the building. With these were modern maps and prints, and all presided over by two plain-coated young men. There is a school for several hundred kept on week-days, and as many on First-day, all poor children. From what I see and hear, the most ample provision is made by the different religious societies for the education of all classes."

10*th mo.* 20*th.*—"Returned from a visit to the Ragged Schools. Here were nearly a hundred children, from two years to fourteen, with clean, happy faces, classed according to their ages and employments; clothed, indeed, in worn and patched garments, but apparently sufficient to keep them warm. We had chosen the time of our visit at the working-hours, from two to four o'clock. In one part of the large room were twenty boys seated tailor-fashion, mending and making clothes under the direction a professor of the trade; on the opposite side were twice as many girls

busily knitting and sewing; in a room adjoining, half
a dozen boys shoemaking; and, near by, fifty little
creatures too small for handicraft work; these were
under the immediate and apparently good care of young
girls of twelve or fourteen; the whole superintended by
a brother and sister, whose devotion, energy, and skill
are most admirable and praiseworthy. Throughout the
whole 'order reigned,' but enforced, unlike that in War-
saw, by only moral power; for it should be noted that
the attendance of the children is entirely voluntary.
The school is situated in the midst of one of the oldest
and most wretched parts of the town, and many of the
children had miserable and worthless parents. Some
were in appearance beautiful specimens of humanity.
As to their mental developments, they were to me perfectly marvellous; the discipline of the streets makes
them *clever* in the English sense. All this, certainly,
is superior to the discipline of a plantation."

24th.—" An invitation to tea at six o'clock and remain till eight, with Mrs. Schimmelpenninck, author of
a 'History of Port Royal.' Her residence is on one of
the fine terraces of Clifton. We were ushered into a
large drawing-room; in a recess lined with an Indian
screen the tea-table was set; on one side was a large
organ, on which Mrs. Schimmelpenninck performs
almost daily; pictures, busts, a small black crucifix,
chairs, sofas, etc., filling up the apartment. Soon
after we were seated, a fine-looking lady, upwards of
seventy, entered, leaning on her companion and a staff.
Her person is commanding, her dress something in
the Hannah More style, particularly the cap, a large
drab-colored cloth scarf over her shoulders; her face

agreeable and her voice pleasant. She welcomed us courteously, and soon we were seated at her handsomely-furnished table. She asked of America, and, finding I was from Philadelphia, of Bethlehem; she is a Moravian, but was educated a Friend. Though an intelligent woman in general, of America she knew comparatively nothing. She asked why the free States allowed masters to reclaim the slaves who touched their soil; and was surprised that Friends would vote for a slaveholder. She spoke of Lady Guion, of the universality of the Spirit of Truth, of its modifications by the mediums through which it passed, comparing it to a light from a fire she once saw in Edinburgh; the light was of every varied tint from the color of the articles consumed. The tone of her conversation was pleasant and instructive. Nothing was said of Port Royal; I alluded to it incidentally, and she smiled and passed to other things. She detained us till half-past eight o'clock, when we took leave, much gratified with our interview with one of the notables of our early day.

"Yesterday we visited some of the oldest parts of the town, through crooked, narrow lanes, walls high and dark, in some places propped apart with beams, that they might not fall together. We saw places which might compare, in antiquity and gloom, though not in dirt, with some of the Italian cities. Indeed, in one of the strange nooks, where we might suppose there would be an accumulation of filth, the cleanliness of the steps and whitewashed walls was remarkable.

"Took tea again by invitation with Mrs. Schimmelpenninck. Staying with her was a young friend, Miss W., whom I tried to disabuse of the idea that the 'New

York Herald' was a reliable journal on Woman's Rights and reforms in general. There was something fascinating in her dignified self-complacency, which, however, it was interesting to me to tilt against in a series of *ultraisms*. The good old lady, Mrs. Schimmelpenninck, heard me complacently, though doubtless with wonder at the strange doctrines and stranger practices of that young country beyond the great deep.

"You will see by the papers the sensation 'Uncle Tom's Cabin' produces here; never was there anything like it. More than a million copies, and the sale still going on. Blessed among women is the author of so much good feeling."

11*th mo.* 28*th.*—"I am asked if I had visited any schools. Not any of the higher-class schools; even in those I imagine they think little of *our* geography, caring about as much for us as we do for Australia; the gold regions there excite more interest now than we, save in Liverpool and the manufacturing towns in the north, and even with them, America is 'America,' which they hear is a great place; but how great, save in extent, they know not. We are not in their thoughts as they are in ours. Just now, however, all the world, from Lord Shaftesbury downward, are interested in the slavery question. Mrs. Stowe has kindled all hearts, and all long to show their appreciation of her, and their interest in the poor slave."

By invitation from Harriet Lupton, Sarah spent a month in Leeds.

12*mo.* 19*th.*—"The evening of my arrival was a great one for Leeds; how great you could scarcely imagine without witnessing the enthusiasm felt for Lord

John Russell. He had accepted an invitation to preside at the annual meeting of the Mechanics' Institute. The largest room in the place was engaged for the occasion, and though the admission was by ticket, it was thought desirable to go three hours before the time to secure a place. At seven o'clock Lord John arrived. When I saw a small man, sixty years of age, I felt the contrast between his appearance and his fame. This man, so many years at the head of the empire, on whose words in Parliament millions hung with interest, knowing how much, of immense importance to them, depended on his utterances, spoke in almost faltering words, so hesitatingly were they at first delivered, with his hands folded behind him or crossed in front. He is highly regarded here, as the man of the people, one who has always been interested for them, and though 'standing by his order,' which they think right and proper, devoted to the elevation of the working-classes. He had not been in Leeds for forty years; then it was on some similar occasion in the interests of the laborer. Now, he comes from his place in Parliament, where twenty-four hours before he had been speaking *for them*, he, the ex-Premier, presides at their humble institution! The people are in ecstasies, rounds of applause, waving of handkerchiefs, cheer upon cheer, testify to their delight. The audience were interested in Lord John, I was interested in them and their proceedings. Three hours were passed in listening to a succession of speeches, from, it was said, good speakers; there was little to call out eloquence. The closing speech, from the celebrated Cruikshank, pleased me most. I had picked him out from those on the platform as the one to illustrate the scenes before us. He 'threw the resolution overboard,' as he said, and took up teetotalism. I liked him for this, in the presence of the other platform dignitaries, who had probably risen from their wine to come to the meeting. He also defended the Duchess of Sutherland from the attacks of the 'Times,' relating to the Memorial to America, and lauded Mrs. Stowe. His speech was good, but his drollery in speech does not equal his drollery on paper. Lord Beaumont, one of the few Catholic peers, also spoke. His position in favor of education for all classes and against what he considers the aggressions of the Papal See has made him popular. In explanation of his apparent inconsistencies, he says he hopes that all England will return to the bosom of the Church, but when all become Catholics, Englishmen must not yield their political rights to the Pope; they contended for these in the times of their former spiritual allegiance, and must not yield them now. Henry Pease, of Darlington, in his plain coat, pleaded for the education of women as the groundwork of all improvement. The audience appeared composed of the same class of persons as would attend lectures of our Franklin Institute, with which this Leeds institution would rank. It is considered among the first in this kingdom."

1st mo. 4th, 1853.—"Yesterday we went to a public tea-party of the Temperance Mechanics' Institute. At five o'clock long, narrow tables were laid in a lecture-room, provided with nice bread and butter, biscuits and sweet bread, in abundance. At these tables four hundred persons were substantially fed. A female—not, in common parlance here, a lady—presided over each twelve cups, and distributed her beverage, good strong tea, most liberally; white sugar in the bowls and *real* cream in the jugs. Fathers and mothers, young men and maidens, and babies, made up the company. They were well dressed, much in the style of our country places. There is less of class distinction in dress here now than of yore. An hour was spent in this social way. Grace and thanks were sung by all the assembly. An invitation was given to a room below; the greater part of the audience withdrew; in a trice the young men pulled off their coats, removed the boards and trestles, and in a few minutes the benches were arranged for the intellectual entertainment of the evening, speeches and music, to which many more came. I was pleased to witness one of these gatherings, though from what I saw I doubted whether the amount of pleasure compensated for the labor. Experienced ones here say it does; that such good meetings cannot be obtained on the fasting principle. My hostesses and their brothers' and sisters' families are almost the only ones in their rank of life here who associate themselves with this movement; though it is generally conceded that much less wine is drunk than formerly, I see it on all tables save those of the families mentioned.

" Every one speaks of the prosperous condition of the country since the free-trade policy was adopted."

1*st mo.* 6*th.*—" Last evening at a dinner-party, on the centre-table were flowers plucked from the open garden,—winter rose, polyanthus, arbutus, a beautiful tree, which bears flowers and fruit at the same time, the flower a delicate white, the berries like a bright, perfectly-round strawberry.

" The British world is interested in the Mrs. Stowe

Penny Offering, and in the Address to America; they cause much discussion here, which seems their great use, that intelligent action may follow, as this effort will soon be over. A Friend from Edinburgh said that the Memorial from Scotland, which is excellent, much better than even the amended English one, was read at the close of Friends' meeting on First-day, and directed to be signed on behalf of the congregation. This plan has been taken in Scotland to procure the public sentiment, instead of going from house to house to obtain signers.

"In company with two merchants of the place I visited the Cloth Hall, a kind of market-house where nothing is sold but cloth, and this unfinished,—that is, without the last dressings. It is manufactured in the country around and brought here, as farmers bring their produce to market. The building forms four sides of a hollow square; each side has a walk down the middle, and stands on which the goods are displayed. Hundreds were in attendance, yet many stalls were unoccupied; the times are so good, the demand for their wares so brisk, that they are sold at the factories before they are brought to market. In many villages within two or three miles of Leeds are mills which send their work into the town. A curious feature of the Irish character was mentioned. The best cloths are always sold to Ireland; the Irish merchants will take no other; it is not worth while to show the kind of mixture of cotton and wool worn here by the poorer classes. The house of one gentleman here sells thirty thousand pounds' worth of cloth a year to one house in Dublin. Flax is spun in large quantities and sent to Belfast to be woven.

"There is still going on, as for some time past in England, discussion on the subject of national education. To my surprise, I find many enlightened people oppose the plan of education by the government in any form, something on the principle of objecting to public provision for the poor, believing that, on the whole, the voluntary system would work best. This is the view of some who are the most anxious for the elevation of the masses, and are doing the most for them. Mr. Ingersoll, the American Minister, has made some strange statements at public dinners here: that fifty thousand children in Philadelphia were educated by the public, the parents being *unable* to pay for them! 'What a state of destitution!' exclaims one. 'Oh, no one is able who can get it done for him,' says another. I am much interested in hearing discussions of this and kindred subjects; they are often presented to me in such new lights, and by those who have made these things their study.

"Much interest was shown at Leeds in the Address from the women of Great Britain to America against slavery. Copies were sent to every chapel, requesting the ministers to ask the women of their congregations to sign, and others were circulated by private hands. Many papers were taken into the neighborhoods of the poor, and few persons were found to need any explanation, beyond the question, 'Have you read "Uncle Tom's Cabin"?' In Leeds alone about twenty thousand names were obtained to two forms of the Address: one, issued from Stafford House, asking for abolition, but not *immediate;* the other, similar in spirit, asking for immediate emancipation. These remonstrances plead in a sorrowing, earnest spirit, and in such a spirit they appear to be signed by thousands of pitying hearts among the toiling and the lowly."

About the end of First month, 1853, Sarah returned to Bristol, and soon after went to London with Mr. and Miss Estlin.

London, 2d mo. 28th.—" The Friends at Leeds wishing some information respecting the Memorial, I offered to call on the committee in London. Entering a bookstore in Bishopsgate Street, I doubted not that I was in the right place on seeing around me pictures of Elizabeth Fry, Joseph John Gurney, and other friends. I was directed to a room above, when, instead of the two or three persons I expected to see, lo! a roomful of about twenty ladies, all, but two or three, Friends. Summoning my courage, I made my errand known to one to whom I had an introduction, was kindly received, and soon was seated in friendly relations with them, they appearing quite pleased to have an American among them, able and willing to give them information on a few points on which they were consulting. The relations of our general and State governments, so simple to us, are as puzzling to them as many of their political arrangements are to me ; sometimes a wheel within a wheel where I least expected it."

3d mo. 24th.—" On the 15th I went to Stafford House, to be present at the last meeting of the Committee on the Memorial to America. As it was the wish of all that the two should be a united affair, the Friends' committee were invited to attend. We were met at the door by servants in the usual livery, passed through a hall and passage to the grand hall, there met by a footman in

complete Highland costume, who conducted us up the
most magnificent staircase I have seen in Europe into
the picture-gallery, where were some twenty ladies.
The Duchess of Sutherland met us, with a kind pressure of the hand, which was also extended to about
twenty more as they came in. On a table were twenty-
six bound volumes of the Address, the Stafford House
one engrossed on an illuminated sheet, with the arms
of Great Britain on one side of the heading, and the
American arms, taken from our coin, on the other.
Half an hour was spent in examination of these and in
conversation among various groups, sitting or standing.
When the company, nearly half Friends, were seated,
the Duchess stood by the table, the Earl of Shaftesbury,
the only gentleman, by her side, and read the report of
the sub-committee, and a letter from Mrs. Stowe accepting the office asked of her, to be the medium of
communication with her countrywomen. Further reports of the committee were read by Lord Shaftesbury ;
the first copy, just procured from the publisher, of the
'Key to Uncle Tom,' the Duchess was asked to accept
from the ladies of the committee. She smiled assent.
Lord Shaftesbury then stated that the Duchess wished
him to say that when Mrs. Stowe came to London she
would be invited to Stafford House, that the Duchess
hoped the ladies of the two committees would meet
her there, with other friends ; this it was thought would
be pleasanter to Mrs. Stowe than a more public reception.
Of course, the ladies smiled their most pleased assent to
such an invitation, happy in the thought of meeting
Mrs. Stowe, and in such a place. Again there were
social groups ; tea, coffee, bread and butter, cakes, and,

alas! wine were handed around; another half-hour spent, our leave-takings were made in the same friendly manner as our reception; indeed, the whole affair was less formal than ordinary parties, though of the same general character. On our retiring, we were shown through the other apartments, drawing-room, boudoir, banquet-hall, all much in the style of other princely mansions, with an air of elegance and comfort; particularly the private sitting-room opening out of the drawing-room, so filled with books, papers, pictures,—private ones of the family,—and the et cæteras of noble work. The picture-gallery was a room about one hundred feet by thirty at a guess, the walls lined with fine paintings, and beautiful sculpture in various places. On one side were three large niches or arches, in the middle one a bright fire in a gorgeous and brilliant grate, surmounted by a magnificent mantel and entablature; on one side a large painting, 'The Return of the Prodigal Son,' on the other, Abraham receiving the angels at the door of his tent, both Murillos, and said to be the finest in the kingdom. One other great ornament must not be forgotten, a group of four fine *live* boys, from five to eight years of age, dressed in the Highland costume, attended by their tutor, interested spectators of the scene before them, 'for the sake of the poor slave.' The Duchess told me two were her sons, the others her daughter's, the Duchess of Argyle.

"The inquiry was made of Lord Shaftesbury what specific dangers he apprehended in America from immediate emancipation, while in their own islands it was peaceful and successful. 'For himself he did not apprehend any, but many others did,' giving the old fears that have been proved, by reason and experiment, to be groundless; 'and the Memorial was written to gain such as these,'—a mistake, I think, but not of great consequence; his 'three years' are considered as immediate, and the great good of the Address is the strong testimony against slavery, which will be felt."

4th mo. 28th.—" Yesterday, in company with Mary Carpenter, the author of the book on Ragged Schools, and one of the most faithful workers among the perishing classes, I walked four miles to Kingswood, where, for the last eight months, she has been much occupied in forming an establishment to receive young vagabonds and criminals. When we entered the gate, eight bright, happy girls, between the ages of twelve and sixteen, were playing and swinging. Several of them came bounding towards Miss Carpenter with a merry laugh and shout. There are nine girls and seventeen boys in the establishment. We saw them at supper; a large slice of good bread on each plate, and a tin cup of milk and hot water. All looked in excellent health. They were collected in the school-room, a number of songs and hymns were sung; then in another room, for more than an hour they highly enjoyed an exhibition of the magic lantern. All in bed by nine o'clock. My visit was on an extra holiday, and I saw all things at their best estate; yet on some accounts I had better opportunities of judging of the scheme. I was taken over the establishment by one of the teachers, of whom I learned much of their trials and difficulties in their efforts to bring under restraint these unruly members of our social order. These have been many, as the plan is to restrain by moral force instead of high walls and bolts.

It is a satisfaction to know that the last month has been the most comfortable one since the commencement. The house and grounds, admirably suited for the purpose, were built and planned by John Wesley for a boarding-school for ministers' sons. With much interest I sat in his study and went through his secluded walk in the garden. Kingswood is in one of the coal districts of England, and the village is inhabited by colliers, it is pleasant to know much civilized since Wesley's day.

"A few days ago we visited the Baptist College in this city; saw many interesting objects in the library. One of the cases filled with some of the oldest Bibles, another with Bibles in different languages; the veritable Concordance which Bunyan used in his prison; an original portrait of Oliver Cromwell, a miniature, for which they had been offered five hundred guineas; two original papers of the 'Spectator,' in glazed frames, not looking so unlike the printing of the present day; a pair of knit cotton gloves—many darns and holes —worn by Queen Elizabeth. This city was a favorite of hers. Brandon Hill, now in the midst of the town, was guaranteed by her forever to the washer-women of the place to dry their clothes.

"At the annual meeting of the Managers of the Blind Asylum, the appearance and performances of the pupils did great credit to themselves and their teachers. Mr. Estlin is much interested in establishing a printing-press, whereby they can print not only for themselves, but for other institutions. He has examined many forms of types used for this purpose, and has decided to adopt the common Roman types. One great objection to the use of any uncommon alphabet is the greater separation from the world around them. They could not go into a graveyard and read the tombstones, which has been found a great *amusement* to them!"

On the 15th of Fifth month she went with the Estlins to London, where she met her friend, J. Miller McKim, from Philadelphia, and for some weeks enjoyed his society, and that of Mrs. Follen and others.

5th mo. 18*th.*—"The meeting in Exeter Hall was a large one, and in many respects great, though the speaking was nothing to boast of, either as to manner or matter. The sight of such an immense mass of human beings is of itself imposing. The Duchess of Sutherland was cheered on entering. When Mrs. Stowe appeared the house came down in rounds of applause; three British cheers were called for and given most heartily. The Duchess took her hand with a look of affection; they stood up together, Mrs. Stowe with calm, unpretending dignity. Soon after Professor Stowe made his speech, late in the evening, Mrs. Stowe withdrew, again cheered."

5th mo. 19*th.*—"Yesterday we attended the annual meeting of the Unitarian Association. Henry Crabb Robinson, an elderly gentleman of high standing in the literary world, not as an author, but their companion and friend, was in the chair. He made some interesting remarks in connection with the subject of American slavery, which was brought up by a resolution asking their brethren of a common faith in America to act in this matter as became their high profession. He said that early in life he ceased to be a Trinitarian, but he had never connected himself with the Unitarians, as he shared the feeling, common in the world, that, though as a society they stood high in intellect and learning, they were not warm in Christian feeling. When staying with Thomas Clarkson he read an address of the Unitarians in England to their brethren in America on the subject of slavery; they both felt and said, 'This is instinct with vital Christianity,' and from that day he was satisfied to join the society. In reference to slaveholders and the apologists of the Fugitive Slave Law occupying the pulpit, he feared that, like the ancient tradition, 'no grass would grow where their feet had pressed.' To one who did not think the association the place and time for the discussion of American slavery, quoting Solomon, 'There is a time for everything under the sun,' he replied that Paul had said there are some things which 'in season and out of season' may be spoken, and was not St. Paul higher authority than Solomon?

" I called on Cornelius Hanbury, Plough Court, Lombard Street, the house and place of business so long identified with the name of William Allen. It was interesting to walk through the plain, venerable mansion, and to dine from the same table which had fed so many worthies now gone to their rest. It was Yearly Meeting time, but on Seventh-day there is no public meeting; the family were at their place at Stoke Newington. Cornelius Hanbury was there; received me politely and kindly, and urged my staying to dine and attend a meeting of the Free Produce Association in the afternoon. Some dozen friends dined with us. The meeting, held in Devonshire House, was a women's meeting, though a few men were present,—Eli Jones,

John Candler, Dykes Alexander, Joseph Sturge. Professor Stowe and Harriet Beecher Stowe were present a short time; both spoke, she in confirmation of her husband's views, and relating a few pleasant incidents in a simple manner."

5th mo. 25th.—" Yesterday, with William Wells Brown, I breakfasted with some friends at the veritable inn of which the Wicksteeds spoke. In the heart of London, in a quiet, clean court, is a large house where at this time one hundred Friends are accommodated. Large rooms handsomely furnished, three of them opening into each other, in the largest a table at which fifty could be seated, two in the next, accommodating as many more; at one of these we sat with our friends. A chapter was read ere we commenced our pleasant social repast. There were some fine-looking young men at our table, and altogether a ' goodlie' company.

"In the evening the British and Foreign Anti-Slavery Society gave a *soirée* to Mrs. Stowe in Willis's rooms; about a thousand persons present, half of them Friends. On a raised platform at one end of the room sat Joseph Sturge, Chairman, the committee and their wives, with Mrs. Stowe and her husband. Samuel Bowley read an address to her, to which Mr. Stowe replied. The company were then invited to walk by the platform, in the front of which she sat, to pay their respects. They were asked, on account of her feeble health, to excuse her shaking hands with them. She bowed pleasantly to persons as they passed, and to some she was particularly introduced, among them William and Ellen Craft, William Wells Brown, and Edward Matthews, these being mentioned in the ' Key.' The company separated in different rooms for refreshments; tea, coffee, etc., in one room, meats, salads, ices, etc., in another; Mrs. Stowe and her party with the committee in a small room. All was over soon after ten o'clock."

CHAPTER VII.

TRIP TO SWITZERLAND.

" NEAR the end of the month, in company with Mrs. Follen, her sister, and son, we went to Switzerland; *via* Dover, Calais, and Amiens, to Paris, where we spent three days, and experienced a disappointment in not being admitted to the Tuileries, by the Emperor coming in from St. Cloud for that one day. It seems written in the book of fate that there is to be no entrance for me to those historic saloons, for each of the four times I have been in Paris there has been some special reason for exclusion; they must remain among the things unseen.

" At Strasbourg we stayed a day, giving ample opportunity to look at the grand cathedral, and to wander through the quaint old streets, with steep-roofed houses, and from three to five rows of dormer-windows. I saw one solitary stork on the top of a chimney, and one flying at a great height, though not so high as the spire of the cathedral, which rises to the sublime. The structure is magnificent. Thence to Basle and Luzerne, where we admired the Lion of Thorwaldsen and the curiously-pictured bridge. A shooting festival, held every two years in one of the leading towns, occurring to each once in twenty-six years, was in progress, and gave us opportunity to see the people of different districts and their variety of costume, chiefly among the women.

"At a hotel about two-thirds up the side of the Rigi J. Miller McKim joined us. A place of places it is. I have a neat, clean room to myself, bed with the whitest of covers, bureau, table, closet. The window overlooks the lake, the green waters of which are surrounded by greener hills—green with grass and pine trees—and high, naked rocks. Back of these, snow-covered clefts of mountains, the peaks of which are bare and rugged, and in the distance the Bernese Alps in their ever-during white. In front of this window I write, oft stopping to gaze on the prospect before me, and to long—for when are we perfectly content?—for those of you who would enjoy it to be with me. The first few days were bright and unclouded; after that we had 'all sorts of weather,' which added to the interest and gave us an acquaintance with mountain life that can be gained only by our remaining fixtures awhile.

"From Interlaken excursions were made with an English party, including a grandson of Lady Byron. Crossing the Wengern Alp, rain came on. After some hours on the summit, having had glimpses only of what we hoped to gaze on all day, we made our descent through rain and mud, many of the places so steep and slippery that had it not been for my young friend Ralph, who devoted himself and alpenstock to my service, my slides would have ended I know not where! The valley of Lauterbrunnen, 'nothing but falls,' as we looked down upon it in our descent from the mountain, in its beauty and rocky surroundings might image the Happy Valley from which Rasselas was so anxious to escape. Gazing on this, though enjoying it highly, I could fully sympathize with him. To be thus rock-bound, though in the midst of the brightest of green and lulled by the sound of many waters, would soon weary, and what must the winter be! I am happy to have made acquaintance with avalanches and glaciers. The sound of the first is much as I had imagined; the glaciers look not so beautiful at a distance, and much more beautiful near to them,—the crystalline, cerulean blue of the crevices and immense blocks of ice. I had no clear conception how they appeared, and now that I have seen them I want to know more, for they do not explain themselves to me. Vevay, Geneva, and Chamouni were visited.

"Our finest excursion was to the Flègère, the view from which combines the greatest amount of grandeur and beauty I have yet seen. The valley of Chamouni at our feet, made more *sweet* by distance in more senses than one. The peasant houses here have no beauty; in short, they are stables with all their appendages. Glaciers in sight, Mont Blanc in full view, and its long line of attendant pinnacles, some snow-clad, some in their bare ruggedness. I have now gazed on all these glories for days, and they have been to me a delight, as has been all Switzerland, with its valleys and its mountains; but at no time have the eternal and the sublime been so fully made visible as in the distant snow-crowned Apennines, first seen from the Tower of Pisa, and afterwards from the windows of the Vatican. Near Geneva we visited Mr. Paget, an English snail fancier. Three hundred specimens of the eighteen hundred existing species he had collected himself since the commencement of the year, while he resided in the south of France."

Bex, 8th mo. 21st, 1853.—"At a ' pension,' with all domestic comforts about us. I read a little, walk a little, and talk a little to the German ladies who speak English. A number of them are familiar with our language and literature; the best authors they know as well as we do. I long that our young folks should have some such mental training as I see around me."

8th mo. 28th.—" I went to the church of the village; the hours here are so early that I did not arrive till after the sermon. In this plain meeting-house five or six hundred men and women—not a child or apparently quite young person in the congregation—sat on benches, the women in front of the pulpit,—placed at the side,—the men apart on either hand. At the close of the hymn half a dozen persons, apparently strangers, went out. I arose also, but as the people remained, so did I. A short address and prayer in French; the minister descended from the pulpit and went to the side aisle, where on a table were the bread and wine of the communion. By this table each man of the assembly passed in slow procession, pausing to take the mouthful of bread and the sup of wine; each then returned to his place, looked a mental aspiration, and took his seat. After this, in order due, came the women, with measured and reverent step. I was interested to witness this ceremonial; once, if not now, doubtless significant to each partaker as the assertion of the right of all to the 'communion of the saints,' not to be prescribed by pope or priest. In this valley were the Waldenses and Albigenses."

Clarens, 9th mo. 1st.—"Truly can I say that these mountains and valleys have been to me a delight, and in their grandeur and beauty exceeded all my imaginings. In some particular things I have been disappointed, but, on the whole, the earth and sky and cloudland are unequalled in my experience."

CHAPTER VIII.

RETURN TO AMERICA.

FROM Clarens Sarah Pugh returned, *via* Fribourg, Berne, Basle, Heidelberg, Cologne, Antwerp, and Calais, to London, arriving 9th mo. 28th. On the 29th she went to Bristol, and on the 5th of 10th mo., in company with J. M. McKim, embarked for New York, where they arrived on the 16th of 10th mo., 1853.

Upon her return after her second visit to Europe she became a member of her brother Isaac Pugh's family, residing in Germantown,—her quarters of rest in the city with her uncle, Isaac Jackson, who, with his two sisters and two nieces, formed a family circle in Green Street above Tenth. As her great interest was in the anti-slavery cause, she was much occupied with the labor required of her as one of the Executive Committee and member of the Female Anti-Slavery Society.

10*th mo*. 17*th*.—She writes, "The Fair Circle met at James and Lucretia Mott's this evening,—about sixty to tea, after which our number increased. More than half were faces new to me, having joined the movement within the last two years. Quite a contrast, this brilliant scene, with our small number, eight or ten, who repaired to a school-room because it was central, each with her supper of nuts and cakes brought in pocket, eaten at twilight while we walked in the yard, —then a few more hours' work by the glimmer of candles."

10*th mo*. 23*d*, 1853. (To an English friend.)—"Our voyage home was boisterous; many of the two hundred passengers were sick. Our opportunities of acquaintance and intercourse with the crowd were of the most perfunctory character; for this I was sorry, as there were many Southerners on board with whom, under favorable circumstances, we should have been glad to mingle. Some were slaveholders, one with her slave,—a fine-looking young colored girl,—others apologizers for the system, and a few defenders of it. One day, in the saloon, I found Miss Cabot lying on a sofa in earnest discussion with two ladies. She told me she listened for some time to their abuse of Mrs. Stowe and her 'money-making' till she could bear it no longer. The first sound I heard was, 'Block! block! yes, that is the way she tells stories, sell them from a block!' Miss Cabot calmly replied that she did not contend for the word, the fact was the same, that the slaves were bought and sold. ' Yes, I know ; *I* will have those I like and *can treat kindly*, and if those I have are bad niggers, I sell them and get others.'

"Our table company, when able to be there, were Colonel Walton, ex-Governor of Florida; his daughter, Mrs. Le Vert, of Mobile, the owner of the slave-girl; Mr. S., a New Orleans exquisite; Mr. Thomas, a hale old gentleman of seventy-three, now a resident of New England, and brother-in-law to Mr. Furness; his son, a merchant residing in New Orleans, *not a slave-holder*, too much of a Northerner for *that*, but one anxious to apologize for them, and to show the best side of their character; admiring Mr. Furness for his conscientious action, but thinking him much mistaken in his views of slavery as well as of theology. He himself was eminently a religious man, according to the common standard, concerned for the observance of the Sabbath, much interested in churches and Sunday-schools. One slaveholder told me she thought 'Uncle Tom' an exaggeration, but candidly added, ' An intelligent friend of mine, who owns slaves herself and has a more extended acquaintance in the South than I have, says it is too true.' On our landing in New York, almost the first things we noticed on the streets were the large play-bills of the theatres announcing the performance of ' Uncle Tom ;' in Philadelphia the same."

10th mo. 24th.—" Through a pelting storm I went with numbers of the ' faithful' to Norristown to attend the annual meeting of the Pennsylvania Anti-Slavery Society. The reports you will see in the ' Freeman,' which cannot tell the exultant feeling of my heart in witnessing the earnest devotion of the tried and true, who for long years have toiled in this cause, still at their posts, and braving the storm to be where duty called. With what delight did I listen to Lucretia Mott detailing in her animated way her meetings in Kentucky, and watch the joyful play of her countenance at the thought that in a slave State she had been able to declare the whole counsel of the gospel of freedom ! and did I not enjoy the freedom of the platform, in contrast with the heavy pressure of Exeter Hall ? Strange as it may seem to you, who can think of this land only as darkened by its giant crime, my abiding feeling, as I gaze upon our blue skies, over the wide-spread landscape, on the broad streets of the city, while inhaling the balmy, fresh air, is of exultation and hope; it cannot be that where there is so much good, evil can long continue in the ascendant. Whatever my feelings in the future may be, they are certainly now not with the desponding party."

12*th mo*. 2*d*.—" Evening, a preliminary meeting for arrangements held in L. Mott's drawing-room. Our New England friends arrived safely, hopeful and happy. Interesting letters read. The one which charmed me most was from Garrison, in reply to an earnest but timid soul, who fears more for Christianity from the infidel *words* of the abolitionists than the infidel *deeds* of the slaveholders."

12*th mo*. 3*d*, 1853.—" The twentieth anniversary of the formation of the American Anti-Slavery Society was held in Philadelphia. W. L. Garrison, Wendell Phillips, Edmund Quincy, and others from New England attended."

12*th mo*. 5*th*.—" Opening of the Anti-Slavery Fair;

admittance twenty-five cents, season tickets fifty cents; three hundred and twenty dollars were taken at the door. The prospect of hearing Wendell Phillips occasioned the rush, and he did speak, to the great delight of some and the horror and scandal of others, who 'had never heard such blasphemy! Why, he spoke against the Church in the most shocking and outrageous manner; what an infidel he must be!' 'Oh, no, not an infidel; he is orthodox.' 'Utterly impossible, or he could never have spoken thus.' 'Nevertheless, he is orthodox according to your own standard.' *Some* of *us* were somewhat scandalized by his denunciation of what he termed 'Quaker non-resistance;' '*that* ought to have been thrown aside, and the slaveholders prevented at the point of the bayonet from carrying into bondage an unborn child,' as was the case in Philadelphia a few years since."

12*th mo.* 6*th.*—"Spent at the fair. Garrison's speech in the evening pleased every one. An orthodox Friend who came from curiosity to see and hear '*the monster*,' was perfectly fascinated. 'Never heard a more impressive and solemn speech;' begged to be introduced to him, to express his great satisfaction with what he had heard. Another, who came expecting to see 'twenty Quakers and a hundred niggers,' was deeply interested by 'the fine faces of the assembled multitude, the thoughtful, earnest expression of the countenances of the women.'"

3*d mo.* 10*th*, 1854.—"I had the great pleasure of hearing H. W. Beecher, a real live man; how thankful I am the world is blessed with some such! Of this kind I think must be the Rev. Mr. Kingsley, whose 'Hypatia' I have just finished reading. His masterly insight into human nature in its diversified manifestations shows a keen, searching, and discriminating mind."

4th mo. 11*th.*—"At L. Mott's accidental dinner-party last week were present Griffith M. Cooper, of New York, a radical abolitionist, once a Friend, now an ultra-liberal; Mrs. Rose, a Polish Jew, now an eloquent speaker on woman's rights and other ultraisms; Mrs. Townsend, a temperance lecturer; Sarah Grimke, a repentant slaveholder, etc., etc.; Mr. Pelham, a Methodist slaveholder from Texas! I was invited to meet Mrs. Rose and Mrs. Townsend, the only ones expected, but I could not go, and missed the earnest appeals of the sturdy Mr. Cooper to his slaveholding brother on behalf of his bondmen. Have we not strange amalgamations?"

7th mo. 7*th.*—"A few days since L. Mott was speaking of the pleasures of the different periods of life; the pleasures in all stages, under ordinary circumstances, she thought far overbalanced the pains. One great pleasure in her present life, now in its later stage, was the feeling that there were younger hands than hers —she particularly rejoices in the Lucy Stones and Antoinette Browns—to contend with the long-standing abuses in the world, and that consequently she did not feel so heavy a pressure of duty upon herself. She must feel, too, though she did not say it, that her life has been spent in the good fight, the blessed reward of which is the 'quietness and assurance' that such labor has not been in vain.

"I hope you will be sorry to miss our 'Freeman,' yet I think you will agree with the majority that we have made a wise arrangement; a *wise* expenditure of means is important to us. Our office and all other machinery are kept as before."

4th mo. 23d, 1855.—" With deep sorrow have we heard of H. Martineau's illness. I feel the prospect of losing her as a personal affliction, so much has she been to me for more than twenty years. Few writers have spoken to me as she has done : her spirit so true, her heart so loving. All her philosophy I do not accept ; her truthfulness to her own convictions is dear to me. Then she was with us and of us in the early days of anti-slavery, and to those who are *ever* true we cling with great fondness."

5th mo. 27th.—" Really, the better times are coming ! as I felt while reading a work by the Rev. Edward Beecher, ' The Conflict of Ages.' The courteous and respectful manner of speaking of Dr. Channing and other Unitarians shows that the bitterness of theological controversy is passing away. This work I read to please a friend, for it is not exactly in my line of reading ; never feeling myself called upon to believe in ' human depravity' and ' original sin,' I have never felt a difficulty in settling their conflicting claims. On finishing the book, I accidentally picked up a new work in which the Quaker doctrines, as held by the Unitarians of that body, were set forth, and after the rocks and quicksands of Presbyterian theology, it seemed like lying down by the ' green pastures and still waters' of a higher life."

10th mo. 17th. (After attending a Woman's Rights Convention in Boston.)—" I heard Theodore Parker preach a grand sermon, ' Wherewith shall a young man *cleanse* his way ?' Not by force, lion and tiger

fashion, as in the infancy of the world; not by ex-
pediency,—rats and foxes; not by law,—Kane and
others; not by honor,—beggars and thieves have honor;
not by public opinion; not by the Bible; but by the
Light Within, though he did not use that term. It
was joyful to see thousands listening with deep attention and beaming countenances to the unfolding of his
great thoughts. The next day went with W. Phillips
to see Parker and his library of eighteen thousand volumes; the largest private library in this country, next
to Everett's. It occupies two large rooms thrown into
one in the third story of his handsome dwelling. The
entrance-door is garnished, not guarded, on each side
by old guns, one the *first* piece taken from the English
in the war of the Revolution. Prints, busts, maps,
flowers, adorn the rooms, in which he appeared as a
workman surrounded by his tools, with kindly gentle-
manliness doing the honors of the place."

In the autumn of 1856, Sarah Pugh left Germantown and joined four of her cousins at 1014 Green
Street in organizing a pleasant home. In their spacious
parlors the business meetings of the Executive Committee of the Pennsylvania Anti-Slavery Society were
held for years. Other gatherings of interest and pleasure made this generous home a place to be remembered
by many.

1*st mo.* 3*d*, 1857.—" Mattie Griffith, author of ' The
Autobiography of a Female Slave,' came North in her
twenty-third year. Born in a slave State, and surrounded from childhood by slaveholding influences, she
became an abolitionist of the ultra stamp, never having
seen an anti-slavery paper till within the past few weeks.

She has proved her faith by her works in liberating a number of her slaves, and only retaining a nominal ownership of others till legal arrangements could be made for their freedom. We have never met one so fully identified in feeling with the slave, and this by no spasmodic conviction, but by a life-long sympathy. The horrors she depicted she knew. On reading ' Uncle Tom' she said, ' Ah, Mrs. Stowe knows only the echo of the system.' Her character is explained by her early life. Losing her mother when she was five months old, she was placed in a cabin with a slave ' mammy' to be nursed; here she remained, in companionship with the children,—some nearly white,—till she was five years old. She heard the wrongs and hardships of the slaves commented upon by the slave instead of the master, and with the instinctive and ready sympathy of childhood made his case her own. The effects of this teaching no after-efforts could efface ; friends and family ridiculed, reasoned, persuaded, called ministers of religion to their aid in ·vain ; she continued firm in her conviction that slaveholding was a crime of the deepest dye. Educated a Catholic, when she found the priest supporting the system, in her own words, ' I left the Church, though I had taken all the sacraments but marriage and extreme unction.' The ministers of the sects thronged round her hoping to gain a convert; they all upheld slaveholding, and ' I told them my religion was anti-slavery.' Her book was written and sent North a year ago."   ·

In the autumn of 1859, John Brown's attack upon Harper's Ferry startled the country, and the succeeding events, culminating in his execution at Charlestown,

Virginia, 12th mo. 2d, 1859, produced a profound impression on the community. Sarah Pugh writes to Miss Estlin:

11*th mo.* 28*th*, 1859.—"The papers tell you of the absorbing thought of our public in connection with ' The Hour and the Man.' Mrs. Brown returned from Eagleswood ten days since, to be as near as possible to the scene of the tragedy now acting before the world, and to do the duty of each day as it may be made apparent. Truly, she knows not what a day may bring forth, but be it what it may, she appears nerved for the trial. She was present at Mr. Furness's Thanksgiving sermon, which was a full outpouring of his true heart on the momentous events of the time. After church many went to take Mrs. Brown by the hand, and by kind pressure or tender word expressed their sympathy. Others stood reverently aside, and only by looks told their deep interest. One sister who had taken her by the hand said to another, ' Why did you not go to Mrs. Brown?' ' I did not feel that I could.' ' And *I* felt that I couldn't *not* go.'

" Yesterday, in Mr. Furness's church, John G. Fee, of Kentucky, gave an interesting account of his struggles. He is a Kentuckian by birth, his parents owning slaves. Sent to Lane Seminary to study theology, he also was taught humanity, and though as painful as to a Jew of old to call himself a Christian, he took the name of abolitionist, as that only expressed the sentiments of his heart, the convictions of his understanding. Through much tribulation (related in no whining tone), he proclaimed through his native State the sinfulness of slavery and the duty of immediate emancipation."

29th.—" Last evening W. Phillips gave his magnificent lecture on the noble Toussaint L'Ouverture ; it was worthy of them both, and of the heroic John Brown, whose character and actions were brought out in full relief, and with a halo of glory that cannot soon fade ; and this was listened to by a sympathizing audience ; great applause, without a murmur of dissent that could be heard."

The fair of 1859 opened as usual, and was largely attended. On the fourth day the mayor directed that the flag bearing the Liberty Bell, suspended across the street, should be removed ; which order, as the enforcement of a municipal law, was obeyed. A few hours later the sheriff, in execution of proceedings by the trustees of the building against the lessee, took possession, and required the fair managers to remove at once. A meeting of the Fair Committee was held in the room, Sarah Pugh presiding with calmness and dignity, still vividly remembered by some of her associates. Another hall was obtained, and the fair was continued the remainder of the week with marked success.

2d mo. 28th, 1860. (To Miss Estlin.)—"Could I have written immediately after and given you a private account of some of the scenes ! But I was worn and tired, and when I thought of attempting it the vision of M. W. C.'s glowing chronicles came before me, and I despaired of imparting interest even to the exciting events through which we have passed : our interviews and discussions with trustees, lawyers, high-constables, and sheriffs ; business meetings of the Fair Committee, all ladies, surrounded by gentlemen, who looked with wonder on the ' irrepressible women,' amazed to see them

so 'plucky,' and declaring they would vote for them
for the Legislature. Such were the comments that we
afterwards heard had been made, while we were engaged in grave debate as to the best thing to be done
under the circumstances. One spectator longed for the
power of making a picture that would be historical."

6th mo. 22d.—"My cousin Abby attended with me
the Anniversaries last week in New York. It was a
comfort to us old stagers to see the large appreciative
audiences of intelligent young folks,—young compared
with the platform worthies, who had occupied their
places time out of mind. There was the venerated
President Garrison; Phillips, whose youthful bloom
and grace have subsided into polished manhood; Purvis
and McKim, with faces that speak of years of earnest
life; Thomas Garrett in decided age. Eight of our London party were present, rejoicing that they had been
counted worthy to be of the elect.

"Mrs. Stanton's speech tells what the anti-slavery
cause has been to her. It was interesting to see the
matron of forty, the mother of six promising children,
the earnest, self-reliant reformer, and recall the bride
of twenty, before whom a new world of thought and
duty was opening, to which she was introduced by as-
sociating with Lucretia Mott, whose intellect and heart
not only prompted her own liberal thoughts and deeds,
but aroused to action, according to their own testimony,
many of England's noble daughters. You would have
enjoyed hearing, in the Woman's Rights meeting, Mary
Grew's eloquent and beautiful testimony to the character of Lucretia Mott, the public reformer, as wife,
mother, and friend, while Rev. George Cheever, D.D.,

listened with curious yet apparently earnest and admiring interest. Rev. Beriah Green, who went off from us with 'New Organization' in 1840, on the woman question, returned after twenty years, delighted to be once more with those whom he felt to be so good and true.

"It was a happy event to see Garrison's look of quiet yet earnest rejoicing as he welcomed back his old friend.

"I have just read two addresses of W. Phillips with great interest and pleasure. One delivered in 1853, 'The Philosophy of the Abolition Movement;' an admirable exposition of our principles and practice, with their results, and worthy of wide circulation; the other, 'The Pulpit,' delivered in Music Hall in November last; never printed in our papers, for it is neither political nor anti-slavery, only in a broad sense. It would please you by its universality and breadth."

10*th mo.* 6*th*, 1860.—"My sixtieth birthday. In a reminiscence of the long vista of years, there is nothing which impresses me more forcibly than the sameness of the character of my mind, the earnest longing for light and truth, the continued sense of inability to accomplish anything beyond the petty trivialities of the day, the dwelling in little things, not from the love of them, but from the want of effort and the feeling of power to escape from them; for these little things must be done to make the lives of others and my own comfortable; and why should I not accept them as *my work*, as gifts for accomplishing greater things are not mine? Not that I crave great things to be accounted great by the world; indeed, no!

"The past ten years have witnessed many external

changes. In '51 my mother left me; no other one to whom I am a special comfort and support, no other one to be my lodestar. Thus placed, what has been my life? Alas! without record, save as one crowned with blessings.

> " ' Through no disturbance of my soul
>   Or strong compunction in me wrought,
>   I supplicate for thy control,
>   But in the quietness of thought :
>   Me this unchartered freedom tires ;
>   I feel the weight of chance desires ;
>   My hopes no more must change their name,
>   I long for a repose that ever is the same.' "
>   ODE TO DUTY, BY WORDSWORTH.

7th mo. 14th, 1861.—" These times call forth many beautiful traits, which are as the silver lining to the black cloud. Thanks to the good Father, nothing is wholly evil. We watch the events of the war from day to day with great interest, but my faith in the peace principle only waxes stronger, though neither Garrison's nor L. Mott's exposition of it quite satisfies me ; not that I could make it plainer to other minds, not having the gift of expression equal to my thought.

" How many noble women we have in the world ! Just now I feel in good humor with them, so cultivated and so useful ; and if Dr. Dio Lewis and his gymnasium fulfil their promise we may hope for something still better in the future ; though I am so much of a utilitarian that I wish all this energy might be used to relieve the burdens of the overworked and toiling masses. That will come in the good time ' foretold by prophets and by poets sung.' "

8th mo. 10th, 1861.—"At the Commencement of Harvard College, Wendell Phillips Garrison, W. L. Garrison's son, graduated with high honors. The addresses were anti-slavery, what would not have been tolerated six months previous. W. L. Garrison was invited to the Commencement dinner,—to which, besides the faculty, only distinguished persons are invited. Imagine conservative Harvard brought to this, for there has been no *going* to them. Mr. Garrison, not accustomed to dinners, did not wish to go ; he was temperance too ; but the friends urged that it was a teetotal dinner ; he must go for the sake of the cause. He went, and was highly delighted ; so the world moves."

9th mo. 5th.—"A volume on Education, by Herbert Spencer, I have just read. I find he is considered the philosophical writer on such subjects in England, but his views are adapted to all places and all situations ; not that they are specially new to us, but they are ' well put.' "

1st mo. 12th,·1862.—"The fair realized thirteen hundred dollars. We were surprised as well as gratified by the money result, and the fair itself was a success in all its parts. The *smooth* working of the machinery, the enjoyment of friends, the good will of the public, all made a fitting finale to the labors of years, for everybody now feels that this will be the last, at least the last that the ' old guard' will work in ; if the younger generation in the time to come feel the need of such machinery, they will doubtless make it, with improvements. This idea was not stated in the report ; it only did not end, as in past years, with recommendations to work for the next one.

" Have you read 'Linda,' the autobiography of a slave-woman, edited by L. M. Child? Yesterday I spent an hour with Linda, feeling that she was a faithful and true witness, a worthy and noble representative of her race.

" The difference of views among good folks impresses the necessity of watching carefully your own judgments. Dr. Gleason said to-day that for twenty years he had not attempted to controvert any one's opinions; before that time he was continually trying to convince every one that the views he then held were right, and of course was continually uncomfortable; now he states his own views, hears the views of others, then lets the matter rest, to work its own way in either mind; so hard is it to say positively what is right and what is wrong. This certainly would spare many unprofitable contentions, but would truth be the gainer on the whole?"

3d mo. 4th, 1862.—" You would have enjoyed the meeting held last night, in the same hall where, on the 2d of December, only two years past, we held the John Brown meeting. A large assembly spite of the weather, presided over by Bishop Potter, and addressed by Dr. Tyng; clerical and other dignitaries on the platform, Henry C. Carey seated by the venerable James Mott, and the Rev. Dr. Brainerd by the faithful J. M. McKim. Miller said it was 'delicious'·to sit in the quiet and have your work done, and well done, by such folks. There has been nothing so cheering for a long time as this meeting and the facts developed."

3d mo. 23d.—" Miss Carpenter's letter was interesting. I wish there was an open door for her to go to

Port Royal, for, judging by her letter, she would labor for the freedmen with loving zeal. Last week I went to see a young lady of ample means just returned from Boston, whither she had gone hoping to be accepted for the work. By years of devotion to the poor and suffering she is eminently fitted to labor with the ignorant and lowly. She yearns to throw herself into this work. At Boston she learned that Mr. Peirce, the Port Royal superintendent, is entirely opposed to women's going there! the state of society, owing to the licentiousness of the army and the low state of morals among the blacks, rendering it an unfit place for women. The entire want of comforts in living, too, would make it a situation of great hardship. Nevertheless, Secretary Chase and the Boston and New York Committees have accepted the services of ten or fifteen women, who have gone thither in faith and hope. Reports from these must be heard before others are permitted to go.

"Candidates are principally of three classes,—one, quite numerous, of accomplished, wealthy young girls, who long for earnest work ; these are set aside, over thirty and under sixty being the limit of age ; another class wish it for the sake of the subsistence and with a wish to do good ; another who wish the work but hate the negro ! The only way of going is by government vessels and at the expense of the government."

2*d mo.* 28*th*, 1863. (To an English friend.)—"You doubtless crave to know the hopes, the fears, the opinions, in which we live and move. Willingly would I send you a faithful record if I could, that you might know us as we now are, at least as well as we know ourselves. Our condition is so strange and unlooked-

9*

for that it is at times difficult to realize who and what we are, in connection with the men and things around us. Our daily life goes on in its accustomed routine; we eat, drink, sleep, visit, and are visited,—ofttimes, however, with the feeling, 'are these realities or dreams?' Again, by the events of the hour, our life is intensified, and we know how earnest are the demands upon us to do what we may for those who claim our sympathy and care.

"The papers show you that we accept the Emancipation Proclamation variously, depending on the temperament as well as the principles of the individual. At our quiet celebration, which was like a meeting of 'the old folks at home,' it was delightful to witness how fully Robert Purvis accepted the Proclamation, and gloried in *his* country. He that had so long felt injured and outraged in his race, nobly leaving the things that were behind, and looking only to the glorious future. M. McKim and M. Grew spoke well, but Lucretia Mott's was the crowning speech, so pathetically exultant, so touchingly earnest that what yet remained to be done should be done with all our might.

"Miller McKim's nominal resignation of his post as our Secretary has only enlarged his field of operations. It is interesting to watch his intercourse with influential persons, who have heretofore held aloof from the fanatical abolitionists; their interest in the revelations of the slave system, new to them, but so familiar to us; their amazement that such things could be; they do not now so perversely shut their eyes, for events are teaching them the things necessary to the salvation of the nation. That this salvation is to be gained by the sacrifice of the young, noble, and beautiful we deeply feel ; all that we can say is, ' Even so, Father, for so it seemeth good in thy sight.' Though not accepting war as the best and highest mode of action, I deeply sympathize with and admire the noble self-sacrifice and devotion so largely displayed by those who know no better way.

" Port Royal, Fortress Monroe, Alexandria, St. Helena, and other places where ' freedmen' congregate, give ample employment to the benevolent women throughout the country, who have formed associations to work for their relief, literally to cover the nakedness of the poor fugitives. The men work for the government, but the old, the sick, and the children must, on their arrival at these posts, depend on the aid of the charitable. Thousands of garments, simple and strong, are constantly sent, many from those who have been outside of our ranks ; they have waked up and feel that they must do something."

3d mo. 15th.—" Last week we heard Theodore D. Weld. We were much pleased, but not exactly as we anticipated. We felt there was great power within, and from what we saw and heard, doubted not that in early life there must have been an effectual giving of it forth to impress and charm his auditors. Now, his lungs are sound,—he has no disease of the bronchial tubes,—but if he speaks extempore, allowing himself to become excited by his subject, the vocal cords swell and prevent any sound above a whisper. To guard against this, when he feels the necessity he resorts to his manuscript as a quietus upon enthusiasm. The reading from this is fine, and was more to my taste than the declamation. Mr. Furness, in a letter to Mr.

Garrison, says, 'I was filled with admiration of his intimate knowledge of the whole letter and spirit of the pro-slavery iniquity, of his own logic and wealth of language, the exquisite propriety with which he uses words, the right word always in the right place; it is like listening to music.'"

6*th* mo. 9*th*, 1863.—"Boker's noble outburst ('The Black Regiment'), and his lines on the 'Cumberland,' show that his appreciation of the negro here goes beyond those whose pro-slavery is made anti-slavery by the crumbling of the old basis, as some one fitly described many of the converts who could not read you off a confession of anti-slavery faith; they know nothing of the history, metaphysics, or principles of our cause, yet will say they are as anti-slavery as Phillips and Garrison.

"'In the midst of life we are in death' is the old saying. May it not be said of these days, 'In the midst of death we are in life,' so full of vitality and energy are the passing days? How often comes to mind, 'Better fifty years of Europe than a cycle of Cathay,'—if the activity be noble,—and how much of it is so, though at times we cannot help feeling that 'the trail of the serpent is over' it!"

10*th* mo. 6*th*, 1863.—"In looking over the record of forty years this may be acknowledged, that some of the questions that perplexed my early life, time has solved; the theology of the past has given way to the light of reason; but still the existence of evil will at times harrow my soul, which cannot *always feel* that 'God is love,' and that his tender mercies are over all his works."

In the spring of 1864 the Green Street household was dissolved, its members forming other associations.

Sarah Pugh spent the summer in Kennett, Chester County, and in the autumn returned to her brother's, which was her home for the remainder of her life.

1st mo. 17th, 1865.—" A good meeting was held last week to influence the community on the question of colored persons riding in our street-cars; we hope it will greatly help to do away with the odious distinction that has so long prevailed. Much work is doing here for the freedmen and the white sufferers in the South. A large party met to make comfortables for the refugees. Eight were made that afternoon by placing six thicknesses of newspapers (!) between covers of old spreads or dresses, run together and somewhat knotted, mattress fashion. Hundreds have been made in New York and sent South. Though somewhat stiff at first, they wear softer, and are much warmer than nothing; paper is proved a good non-conductor of heat. Now that wool and cotton are so dear, it is wonderful how much is brought forth, both new and old, from the housekeepers' stores and made available for good."

2d mo. 22d, 1865. (To an English friend.)—" On this day, bright and glorious in the sky and on the earth, hallowed by the nation with the memory of the departed, welcomed with the joyful acclaim of bells and cannon for the victory of the present,—Charleston restored to the Union,—jubilant with hope for the future, my thoughts turn to my dear friends abroad, with the wish that they, sharers in our tribulation, could also be sharers of our joy. At high noon I chanced to pass our Independence Hall ; the clock struck the hour, immediately burst forth a joyful peal from the belfry ; not from the ' Old Bell,' ' Proclaim Liberty throughout all the land unto all the inhabitants thereof!' but with almost the assurance that very soon this glorious anthem might be rung over a redeemed nation. Since the passage of the bill for the amendment of the Constitution, we confidently hope that our anti-slavery organizations may soon come to an end, the work to which they were devoted being accomplished. Yet shall we not love to linger over the past, which, with its many trials, has been so rich in all that ' gives life to live' ? What blessed memories cluster around those years! When I contrast my own life with that of many of my early companions, endowed with all that the world gives of wealth and position, and what these command, how poor seems their lot compared with mine !"

3d mo. 1st.—" My rhapsody was interrupted, but I will send it as a mood of the time which you can understand ; for though the end is not yet, and the final struggle may be fearful, beyond it is the glorious future for us, for the world. You will see by the report of the Philadelphia Female Anti-Slavery Society that it is in a cheerful state of mind in these, it is to be hoped, its latter days. Would that you could see it ere it departs! Not that it would be much to look at,—a few aged worthies in a small room,—but you would regard them with loving interest for their works' sake.

" We are reading with interest Miss Cobbe's ' Broken Lights.' What specially pleases me is her manner of dealing with the various theological creeds, the reason of their acceptance by different classes of mind,—different by natural organization and education,—according with human nature and sound philosophy."

3d mo. 30th, 1865.—" Miss Peabody has just returned from Washington. At the President's reception on the evening of the 4th, Frederick Douglass and daughter entered behind her party. Mr. Lincoln looked weary and worn; the crowd was received mechanically, apparently passing before him as shadows in a dream. When he saw Frederick Douglass his kindly eyes lighted up; grasping both his hands, he said, 'I am glad to see you, Mr. Douglass. I will ask you what I have asked no other, how did you like my address?' 'Mr. President, it was *holy*,' was Douglass's happy response. Did it not gratify you that such an acknowledgment as was therein made to the law of righteousness should come from the President? Then he seemed to be worthy of his position as the head of the nation,—a nation which with him has learned, however slowly, that only in justice can a true and lasting peace be established in the land."

At the annual meeting of the American Anti-Slavery Society, in 1865, a proposition was submitted by Garrison to dissolve the society, as the constitutional amendment prohibiting slavery had passed Congress, and was ratified by a sufficient number of States to insure its adoption. Notice having been previously given in the "Liberator" that it would be offered, Wendell Phillips dissented, taking the ground that until the adoption of the amendment should be officially proclaimed it could not be legally enforced, and that while the spirit of slavery was still rampant, and the freedmen had not been granted the right to vote, the work of the Anti-Slavery Society was not finished. These views created an earnest debate in the Society, which to some appeared acrimonious instead of joyous, as was wished. The proposition was rejected by a vote of one hundred and eighteen to forty-eight. Sarah voted in the minority.

7th mo. 3d, 1865.—"The last meeting of the Society should have been harmonious and jubilant instead of divided; the body of the meeting acted in good faith. My personal intercourse with all was most pleasant. Phillips's winning smile, Quincy's playful, pungent wit, Garrison's joyous seriousness, May's bland moderation, Johnson's faithful devotion, Pillsbury's sombre persistency, the Fosters' captious truthfulness to their own ideal, added to the interest. The 'Standard' is so despondent and alarming, instead of cheering and hopeful, it is not pleasant reading; it may be wholesome; time will prove.

"I passed a few hours with Mrs. Frances Shaw, mother of Robert G. Shaw, of the Fifty-fourth Massachusetts (First Colored Regiment), who fell on the ramparts of Fort Wagner, and by the rebels 'was buried with his niggers.' Such a mother and such a son are among the noblest of human kind. I read with intense interest the memorial volume printed, not published, the public documents and private letters relating to her son and his regiment during the eventful three months of the summer of 1863. A daughter is the widow of Colonel Lowell. This noble family is one among many in our land who have endured martyrdom that the slave might be free and our country redeemed. Blessed and holy are they in their sublime self-renunciation."

8th mo. 11th, 1865.—"I have read Theodore Parker's life with great interest and edification. How faithful he was to his highest ideal, and how earnestly he labored to clear the rubbish from the pathway of others! When

I see how huge the mountains are before some, I regard with increasing love and veneration dear old George Fox. From what 'grievous burdens and hard to be borne' has not his simple doctrine of the Inward Light redeemed us! That his followers have mystified and made it of none effect by their traditions takes naught away from his simple greatness. Where one Samson-like mind, as Parker's, breaks the strong cords with which it is bound in early life, how many are fettered and crippled their whole lives long!

"With advancing years I have become less interested in speculative opinions. If this growing indifference extended to practical piety, or did I feel less interested in the welfare and happiness of my fellow-beings, I should be alarmed ; as it is, my heart shrinks from this isolation, this difference in opinion from most of those I love and esteem. Feelings and opinions that many of these deem valuable beyond any earthly treasure are to me as the penance of the ascetic, the dreams of the visionary, or the ravings of the maniac. Why it is thus I know not; if their faith and hope are not 'cunningly-devised fables,' will not an evidence of the truth be granted to one who has not willingly re-jected that heretofore offered? Will not the knowledge necessary to life eternal—if it is something beyond doing justly and loving mercy—be clearly taught by One who delighteth not in the death of him that dieth? It has been said they have Moses and the prophets ; yea, they will not believe, though one rose from the dead. No, that would not confirm my belief; with my present feelings it would be no more than the trick of the juggler. Internal evidence can alone satisfy me.

" Were it not that I wish these scraps to be true mementos to myself of the state of my mind, I should shrink from thus recording them ; even to myself it is hard to acknowledge this want of fixedness on what are considered points so essential."

In the spring of 1866, Sarah Pugh and Abby Kimber visited the South to see the work among the freedmen. A week was spent in Georgetown, District of Columbia, and in viewing the sights of Washington, including the Freedmen's Barracks and the relief and educational work there. Thence "on to Richmond," where, in succession, the Freedmen's Bureau, the Freedmen's Relief, the burnt district rapidly rising from its ruins, Libby Prison, etc., were visited. At Charleston they were met by Reuben Tomlinson, a former associate in the Anti-Slavery Society in Philadelphia, then United States Superintendent of Schools in South Carolina, who assisted them to see what they wished. They visited Wadmalaw Island at the mouth of Edisto River, where the mansion of the former proprietor was occupied by United States military officers, and as a school for freedmen.

4th mo. 10th.—" We visited one school, over six hundred children, in Zion Church, of which Mr. Gibbs is pastor ; with him and the school we were much pleased. He greeted us as old friends, having been a boy in Philadelphia in the early times of anti-slavery. ' You see before you the result of some of your labors; the seed then sown is now being multiplied a hundred-fold.' A school at Mount Pleasant, on the opposite side of the harbor, and that on Wadmalaw, are under the care of Pennsylvania ladies. In another large school, besides the children, we were particularly attracted by the teachers, with whom we dined and spent the remainder of the day in their ' Home,' the former residence of Barnwell Rhett! My admiration of the devotion of these teachers increases the more I see of them. None of them talk of sacrifices, only of their interest in their work.

" In this school are seven lady teachers, all from New England, with the culture and refinement of that region. They, with the principal of the school, Mr. Sumner, make a family home, the ladies taking turns weekly in housekeeping. In their apartments it was interesting to see New England thrift and contrivance overlying Southern magnificence and inefficiency."

Charleston, 4th mo. 14th.—" Yesterday we visited the Normal School. The advanced classes are the children of the free blacks, for whom some degree of schooling was possible before the war. They now occupy one of three elegant and spacious buildings erected for the whites.

" The Orphan Home for the Freedmen occupies a large mansion, before the war the dwelling of Memminger. The place is well suited for its present occupants, some hundred, well cared for, who were found without protectors. We took tea and spent the evening at the Teachers' Home. Miss Hosmer was there for a few days. Her place of labor is a village twenty miles inland ; her plan is to gather together the children of the poor whites and the freedmen. So far her experiment is successful, the children helping one another ; the blacks more vivacious, the whites more cleanly.

" At our family table are United States officers of the

bureau and army; a planter, who was four years in the rebel army; a storekeeper of the city, etc., etc. The conversation, begin as it may, generally gets upon the war, its incidents, the state of the country, past, present, and future; always conducted in good temper and with freedom, avoiding offensive terms, though the words rebel and rebellion are not unfrequently heard. The planter, though a rebel once, we like; he accepts his situation so cheerfully, determining to make the best of it. He is a cotton-planter, has just got his seed in the ground, and is hopeful as to the result.

"To-day has been devoted to the meetings of colored people. In the morning a Methodist congregation in a large school-room, the sermon by a white man. The people presented a variety of hues, ages, and appearance; the old aunties with their turbans and neat white neckerchiefs, younger ones in modern styles; all neat, and many tasteful. Afternoon, to the Episcopal church, the 'upper ten' of the free colored; they were well and fashionably dressed. Their pastor, regularly settled over them, is a Seabrook, from Edisto. An excellent sermon, one that the most cultivated congregation might have enjoyed; he did not appear to be preaching over the heads of his audience."

23*d.*—"Yesterday the great event of opening the Methodist church for the colored people took place. The building, a fine one, had belonged to the white Baptists; no longer able to hold it, the present congregation, aided by friends in the North and others, purchased it for twenty-six thousand dollars. The day was fine, great numbers attended, respectably dressed, their earnest, happy faces giving assurance that they thought the 'good time' had at last come for them. The services were conducted by white and colored persons; their pastor heretofore, as the law required, is white, and appeared to be an earnest, true man. Many white persons attended on this occasion, and a cordial invitation was given them to share the blessings now enjoyed. In the afternoon we went to a fashionable white church; as it threatened rain, few of the chivalry were present. Their house, like most buildings in Charleston, bore marks of the bombardment. The room in which I write has three mended places in the ceiling, one quite large, and more than twenty in the floor; the rooms below have the same appearance; the houses near are patched on the outside, one joining the back buildings was entirely demolished; and this in the heart of the city, several squares from the burnt district. Charleston might be a more beautiful city than Philadelphia proper; the wide piazzas and balconies amidst the trees are more imposing.

"From Charleston by steamer to Beaufort, South Carolina, thence by row-boat to St. Helena Island. Here we found the primitive, unadorned freedman in his first stages of advancement. His starting-point is not now to be found, though from what we hear and see, we fancy we have some conception of it. We were driven a few miles to Miss Towne's and Miss Murray's, 'Pennsylvania Freedmen's Relief School, No. 1,' on the outside. We found over a hundred scholars, from six to twenty-six, both sexes, all shades of black, mostly dark; a number of married women. We witnessed the closing exercises, singing, etc., and then were driven by the ladies six miles to their home in the village, a real home to us in this land. What a home it is to one accustomed, as Miss Towne has been, to the comforts and luxuries of civilized life! Two days we spent in the school, driven there each morning six miles through woods and cotton-fields, the cotton a few inches high. Recess and lunch about two o'clock, school closed at four, then a drive home to dinner at seven. This is their daily routine of school-life. The Easter holiday begins to-day. Early this morning we saw ten men, women, and children waiting in the yard for medicine and other comforts; now others are thronging in, as this is the day set apart for receptions. After the labors of the morning, our hosts drove us ten miles to dine. The drive home by moonlight, unlike the hot mid-day one, was pleasant. We sometimes call at a cabin and talk with the inmates, wondering at their former squalor and destitution, now passing away, but leaving its traces. First-day at church, a clean, tur-baned congregation on the women's side. An earnest sermon from a black brother, more interesting than the learned one heard last week from the white orator of Charleston. After the service three couples were married.

"Our next point was Port Royal Island, where friends from Philadelphia are teaching. Here we made an excursion, more than an hour's row, to the Barnwell plantation, to see the most magnificent live-oaks in this region. Magnificent indeed, long avenues of them, fitting entrances to old baronial castles; at the end of these were dilapidated old houses, in their best estate more rude and rough, architecturally, than many Northern stables. Now, with unglazed windows and unhinged doors, they are the abode of many families that, in the stead of owls and bats, have taken possession, and in future generations may be replaced by fitting mansions for such grand approaches.

"Returned home *via* Beaufort, Charleston, Richmond, and Washington, after an absence of two months."

In the autumn of 1866 the question of disbanding the Pennsylvania Anti-Slavery Society was discussed at its meeting, and the majority decided to continue. A new movement had begun, for Equal Rights, advocating suffrage without distinction of sex or color. Sarah writes : " When, a year since, it was proposed to include women in this agitation for suffrage, I felt that it might be well to stand aside and wait till the black man's rights were secured. I do not feel so now; the black woman's rights are as important as the black man's, and she is in great danger of being specially tyrannized over by him, should he have the power. Robert Purvis magnanimously said, ' *I* should be ashamed to ask woman to stand aside that I might obtain my rights a few years sooner, when she is more oppressed than I am.' A meeting held in Philadelphia in First month, 1867, was attended by two hundred or more persons, mostly the old anti-slavery friends and colored people, yet of a character to give hope that some would be efficient laborers in the good work. The meeting was interesting and spirited, with Susan B. Anthony, Elizabeth Cady Stanton, Lucy Stone, and Henry B. Blackwell. The two last named are an earnest and devoted couple, working harmoniously and with much personal sacrifice in this cause. Henry Blackwell has given up his business for one year to work in New York State before the meeting of their Constitutional Reform Convention. Lucy is earnest and effective as of yore in speaking to thoughtful souls, though the charm of youthful freshness and Bloomer dress has departed. It was a pleasure to hear three such earnest, devoted, well-informed women speak with their wisdom and power; it inspires hope for the sex and for the world."

A festival held in Philadelphia at this time brought together many of the old anti-slavery friends, much to their gratification.

Germantown, 1st mo. 5th, 1868.—" The world moves onward and upward, or this year of grace 1868 would not have witnessed Mary Grew preaching to a Unitarian congregation in this conservative place, and with great acceptance, spite of the fears of friends and the forebodings of those who thought her wandering from her sphere. I had not before heard her from the pulpit, from which she spoke with an unction and power that silenced cavilling. The expressions of satisfaction and admiration were gratifying to hear."

On the 26th of First month, 1868, James Mott passed away. His departure was a great grief to his many friends. It struck a keen pang to Sarah's heart, from her long and intimate friendship with him.

In First month, 1869, in company with Lucretia Mott, she attended a Woman's Rights Convention in Washington, District of Columbia; and in Fifth month, in Boston, Woman Suffrage, Anti-Slavery, and Free Religious meetings, the last, presided over by O. B. Frothingham, was addressed by Christian, Jew, Spiritualist, and Theist, with wondrous fulness of thought and feeling in the speakers and audience. " You recognized the theological element of New England life, as portrayed by Mrs. Stowe."

12*th mo. 5th*, 1869. (To a friend).—" Thy taking ' The Revolution' is much to me, for my heart is in this work for women, as the best work for humanity. *Our* day for *field* work is past, though with strength as formerly, I with thee ' should rejoice in the earnest work of the movement ;' we can make an effort in the chimney corner by rousing and encouraging the younger people to labor. For this the ' Revolution,' with its visits, is an inspiration and a help."

12*th mo. 7th*, 1869.—" You will see how the medical students and, worse still, the professors of our city have been making fools of themselves over the attendance of the clinics by women students. Dr. Ann Preston, the strong little woman, has done good service in the cause by her actions and by the lucid and telling productions of her pen." ·

12*th mo. 25th*.—" I have received from England a tract by Francis Newman on the terrible social evil. All honor to the man who can so bravely place himself in the forefront of the battle which must be waged to redeem society from this foul crime."

1*st mo. 27th*, 1870.—" The Washington Woman Suffrage Convention I hear was a success. The audience before the Judiciary Committee was satisfactory so far as courtesy and a respectful hearing went; the result is yet to be proved. Mr. Sumner is reported to have said that in the twenty years of his public life he had not seen more interest manifested by a Congressional committee on any question, nor a cause more ably presented by its advocates."

2*d* *mo.* 23*d*, 1870.—" I have lately read Lecky's 'Progress of Civilization from Augustus to Charlemagne.' It is a rich mine of information on, to me, the most interesting subject, Man, for

> ' The God, whate'er misanthropy may say,
>   Shines, beams in man with most unclouded ray.'

Or I would say that behind the clouds by which he is surrounded the pure fire burns."

3*d* *mo.* 29*th*, 1870.—" It would have been an enjoyment to thee to be present at the ' Euthanasia' of the Female Anti-Slavery Society. The President's face was perfectly radiant, a ' visible halo of sanctity' was around her; and the Secretary read her admirable report with those exquisite intonations of voice so fitting the words. I wished all interested could *hear* her. What pleasant memories will linger around the old organization with those who were a part of it! For myself, it has been a great privilege and happiness."

10*th* *mo.* 6*th*, 1870.—" The days of our years are threescore and ten; and if by reason of strength they be fourscore, yet the Psalmist's judgment of the remaining days may not always apply. Hitherto my life has so abounded in blessings, that I will not cloud the present by anticipation of the dark days that may not come. At the end of these seventy years I feel as intensely as at any period of life its great mystery. More and more beautiful this world appears, clouded as it seems with sin and suffering. As in my early years my wish was to alleviate these, so now the feeling is intense, with the same consciousness of inability to bless mankind. Yet my faith is strong that the tendencies of the race are ' onward and upward,' and that the Lord God Omnipotent is full of loving-kindness and tender mercies."

2d mo. 27th, 1871.—" Early in the year a convention was called to meet in Washington, by Mrs. Hooker and others, independent of either existing Woman Suffrage organization. Mrs. Hooker went to Washington a week previous to prepare for the convention. On the morning of the meeting a hearing was granted by the Judiciary Committee of the House. In the anteroom they met Mrs. Woodhull, to whom a hearing had also been granted ; neither party knew the other, nor of the efforts each had been making to obtain a hearing. Mrs. Woodhull had been in Washington a month endeavoring to interest members of Congress and the Judiciary Committee. The committee appointed the same hour to hear both ladies. Mrs. Woodhull read an address she had prepared on the political side of the question, Mrs. Hooker spoke on the moral aspects, and Mr. Riddle, an eminent constitutional lawyer, was also heard. Majority and minority reports were sent into the House, where the question was debated and lost, but the minority vote was so large that the friends of the measure were jubilant.

" The convention was in one sense a success, thousands attended, crowding the largest hall in the city. A National Committee was appointed, three members, Mrs. Hooker, Paulina W. Davis, and Josephine S. Griffing, remaining in Washington. The use of a committee-room in the Capitol was granted them, where for several hours daily they received members of Congress and others who wished further instruction in the faith. From all accounts the interest aroused is marvellous, and the belief is expressed that the franchise will come sooner than the most sanguine have hoped."

3d mo. 12th, 1871.—"It is cheering to think of the many agencies now active in the world to enlighten and redeem it from ignorance, crime, and suffering. If one did not believe in progress in good, life must be a sad puzzle. There were great and good beings in times past for whose lives we are thankful, but the standard of goodness in this day for the multitude is much higher."

Sarah's friend, Abby Kimber, died in Third month, 1871. The severing of this tie was keen sorrow. From early life they had been closely associated ; the diversity of their dispositions, with similarity of tastes and interests, strengthened the bond.

5th mo. 14th, 1871.—"I attended, in New York, meetings of both branches of the Woman Suffrage movement. My hope that by going some differences I wished to understand might be solved was not realized, but I am satisfied that I went, and feel that I can work with all who are striving for the desired end, and that end becomes more important in my eyes. Woman's equality with man in every relation of life may redeem and regenerate the race."

8th mo. 20th, 1871.—"Is it not a true saying, ' Where sin abounds, grace does much more abound'? Corruption is rampant, but saints go forth to the conflict, and some day will be victorious. This faith I strive to cherish."

1st mo. 29*th*, 1872.—"When one looks at the mountains of iniquity and oppression in the world, one's heart fails, until cheered by the thought of the glorious host who battle for purity and righteousness. Our Woman Suffrage societies are doing earnest work, each in its own way, the best, perhaps, that each can do. The conventions at Washington this winter were successful in interesting and educating the community. The meeting here, in the early winter, of the Pennsylvania Woman Suffrage Society affiliating with the Boston wing, did good service. Lucretia Mott and myself 'assisted' it by our presence, not otherwise; the exclusiveness was not in accordance with our feelings or our principles. The late convention in Washington, though we could not attend, had much more of our sympathy; no earnest worker excluded from its platform."

5th mo. 24*th*, 1872.—"What I saw at Swarthmore College inspired me with hope that the coming generations of the Society of Friends would not only be worthy of their forefathers, but would add to the faith and works of that noble band the usefulness and beauty of a higher culture than was possible in the early days of Friends. I crave for this society, which I cannot but feel is *ours*, though we are not *now* within its fold, to arise and shine in its primitive strength, showing forth to the world the principles of truth and freedom, in such wise as to attract those who are seeking for a higher and nobler life than is to be found either in fashion on the one hand, or asceticism on the other."

10th mo. 6*th*, 1872.—"I have just finished reading a sermon by Robert Collyer, 'The Two Harvests,' full of brightness and good cheer, just what such a day as

11

this endorses; and though we feel that 'passing away' glows on every leaf and every circumstance around us, yet we will rejoice in each while it lasts, with the hope that what next comes will be well, even as these have been.   This day is to me one on which to number my blessings, and to feel that they have been a thousand-fold beyond what I could ask.

> ' And so the shadows fall apart,
>   And so the west winds play,
>   And all the windows of my heart
>   I open to the day.'

Our dear Whittier!   How often and how fully he gives words to thoughts that burn within us!"

1*st mo.* 26*th*, 1873.   (To Miss Estlin.)—" A convention to amend the Constitution of our State is now in session in this city.   The Committee on Suffrage courteously granted two evenings to hear the petitioners. Five societies wished for a hearing.   One evening 'The Woman's Rights Society of Pennsylvania' and the society from Pittsburg were heard; the next evening 'The Universal Suffrage Society,' the 'Radical Club,' and a representation from the working-classes.   Such was the interest that thousands who wished it could not get tickets of admission; the hall would only accommodate a few hundreds besides the members of the convention.

" The National Suffrage Society held its annual convention in Washington last week.   The interest was great among Congressmen, their wives, families, and the public; the attendance large.   The last meeting, held in the evening, was broken up by a policeman—

doubtless incited thereto—on the pretext that it was illegal, a law of the District requiring a license for an exhibition (!) where money was taken at the door."

2d *mo. 9th*, 1873.—" More than a week of the Constitutional Convention was given up to the subject of Woman Suffrage. Those in attendance report great interest, some excellent speeches on the right side, and some miserably coarse ones on the other. One of the members in opposition said, ' The worst of it is, they have all the *argument* on their side,' and from the reports of speeches we should think it was so ; ' trails,' ' babies,' ' low voting polls,' the strongest points brought forward. Their weakness aids the strength on our side."

In the spring of 1873 a few women of Philadelphia, wives, mothers, and teachers, aroused to their responsibility in influencing the morals of the rising generation, formed a " Moral Education Society ;" the constitution of which declared its object to be " to seek to promote a better knowledge of the laws of being, moral and physical ; to furnish such instruction to children and youth that the coming generations may be better fitted for purity of life and the duties of parentage ; to create a public opinion which shall hold man and woman equally to the highest standard of morality ; to seek the enactment and enforcement of such laws as will tend to the elevation of society and the removal of vice." Sarah took much interest in this movement, and diligently attended the meetings. She assisted in circulating documents and petitions against a proposition in the State Legislature to license prostitution. This threatened legislation was happily prevented by the efforts of the society and others who co-operated with them.

8th mo. 16th, 1873.   (To Miss Estlin.)—"Thanks for the cartes of your noble Mrs. Butler, so instinct with her strength and devotion.   Few in our region know aught of the C. D. work; the need in that direction has not reached us, though from Chicago and St. Louis we hear the rumblings of the storm.   A call for a Congress shows an awakening to the demands of the hour, and the wish to meet them.   In my advanced years it is a great happiness to see this stirring of the waters for the healing of the nations, to know that young and able laborers are giving themselves to the work of the day.   It is a pleasure to aid, if it be no more than encouraging others to enter the field of reform; the labor will be its own 'exceeding great reward.'"

1st mo. 25th, 1874.—"My reading this winter has been principally old books and papers; not very profitable, perhaps.   Sometimes I think to read no *new* books, in another mood no *old* ones; so much in both that I care not for, and so much in both that I do.   I take up Emerson and Whittier and am satisfied; then come the papers and periodicals of the day, and the present and its living interests are all-absorbing."

3d mo. 13th, 1874.—"The estimates of John Stuart Mill's character differ widely; all, however, grant him greatness, and most, goodness, although they may not be in entire sympathy with some of his views of right. Much as I admire him, Mazzini, whose life I have just read, more nearly touches my feelings.

> 'Ah, yes, when all is thought and said,
> The heart still overrules the head.'

Such true principle, devotion to Italy for the sake of

mankind; not simply a patriot as Kossuth, but a world-embracing humanitarian."

4th mo. 19th, 1874.—" What a strange movement is this praying crusade! Good, doubtless, will come out of it, if not to the extent and in the direction that the earnest souls look for. The action of women in this way, and in the Granges, will reveal to them their hitherto unused powers.

. . . "The 'Social Evil' question in our State—the fact of the horrible bill, degrading in its details, passing to a second reading at Harrisburg!—has brought forth many noble protests ; see the list of reverend signers of the letter to Anna E. Dickinson. So far as we can judge from reports, she has risen to a high position in this effort."

6th mo. 28th, 1874. (To M. A. Estlin.)—" I sent you a paper containing an abstract of a lecture by Anna E. Dickinson on the 'Social Evil.' Our State Legislature threatened us with a license law, against which our Moral Education Society sent remonstrances numerously signed. One was signed by thirty of the first physicians of our city. The abominable bill did not pass, but may come up again next winter. We shall not cease to strive and cry and make our voice heard in the streets. Anna E. Dickinson's effort was a brave and noble one, which she rose from a sick-bed to utter."

7th mo. 12th, 1874.—" When young I read history for the facts, the philosophy was beyond me, save in its most obvious sense. It had a great fascination for me, as biography has now. Man has always interested me more than ' bugs and things.' Abbott, of the ' Index,' was in Philadelphia last week. He interested us much by the strength of his convictions and the earnestness of his faith that the superstitions of the present would pass away, though those who now fight against them must labor and wait with what strength they may for the time when light and freedom shall cover the earth 'as the waters cover the sea.'"

2d mo. 13th, 1876.—"Wendell Phillips's lecture I heard. It was well that he began hopefully for the country, for the next Centennial, or we should have been overwhelmed by the picture he gave of the present condition of things among us. My ground of hope for the future has long been looking back on the past, so much has been gained for humanity. 'From seeming evil still educing good,' or, as the present phrase is, 'evolving.'"

4th mo. 27th, 1876. (To M. A. Estlin.)—"Our small Moral Education Society is doing what is in its power to stay the avalanche of evil that threatens to overwhelm us at this time,—foreigners preparing houses of assignation for their countrymen.

"How the 'New Abolitionist' has cheered me! Light seems to be breaking through the dark cloud. I devoured the book, and am now sending it on its missionary way. Josephine E. Butler will stand high on the roll of saints. Elizabeth Fry, Florence Nightingale, and others have done virtuously, but 'thou excellest them all' will surely be her welcome into the noble army of martyrs."

7th mo., 1876.—"I attended the first public meeting in this city of the English agents, Messrs. Gledstone and Wilson, to which women were invited. Our

'Christian Association,' a rich and influential body, have taken hold of the subject; we rejoice in this, though they have not yet risen 'to the height of this great argument,' but they will grow. The meeting was held in the class-room of a Methodist church of respectability and standing; the pastor, worthy of his place, deeply interested; several hundred present, to most of whom the subject was new.

"In this our Centennial year so much demands the time of residents here, visitors to the Exposition from near and far claiming our hospitality, that many subjects which interest us can obtain only a divided attention. Yet we feel that it is well that questions of vital importance to humanity should be considered here and now; the audiences will be drawn from so wide an area that truth will be sown broadcast. One of my special interests is Woman Suffrage, a means to obtain reforms for the future. The National Woman Suffrage Association has opened spacious parlors in a central situation with success; callers through the day from many parts of the country. Yesterday I met there persons from Boston, California, Ohio, Senators' wives and daughters, besides numbers from our own city. All jubilant over the action of the Cincinnati Republican Convention to nominate a candidate for President on a memorial sent by the National Woman Suffrage Association asking for recognition as voters. The appeal was presented by George F. Hoar, of Massachusetts, courteously received and referred to a committee. Mrs. Spencer, of Washington, appointed to present it, 'heard with sympathy;' a generous round of applause twice repeated at the close! This from a 'Tribune' correspond-

ent, inserted in the paper without an editorial sneer as
in times past. The world moves; and who are the
movers? Earnest, true-hearted persons, however they
may occasionally err by overzeal or want of discretion.
M. W. Chapman used to say in anti-slavery days, 'Of
course we want all the virtues on board, but Prudence
is the one we can best spare.' When now I look on
the two wings of the Woman Suffrage movement, I see
on one side the energy, the devotion, the self-sacrifice
that *dares*, and *dares*, and *ever dares;* and on the other,
the conservative caution that avoids even to mention a
successful and triumphant move of the other. The
work of both is doubtless needed, but one is sorry to
see any petty jealousy mar the beauty of either."

11*th mo.* 17*th*, 1876.—"The Centennial is past. The
lessons of this summer have been rich and varied. All
who have been blessed with a sight only of the Fair and
its surroundings must feel an enlargement of heart, intellect, and sympathies; 'the teachingest place,' as said
a visitor. How pleasant it will be years hence, for
those now young, to talk over the exhibits and the experiences of this summer! One of my great rejoicings
is the impetus it has given to women; the Congress was
a great interest."

1*st mo.* 22*d*, 1877. (To Miss Estlin.)—"The Conference in London (on Social Purity), how cheering!
The Continental workers to aid you, their 'good hearts'
so aroused. As to the Congress at Geneva, I rejoice
unspeakably in the position which women will hold
there in contrast with the Anti-Slavery Convention of
1840; good for women at large as well as for the work
in hand. Our society here continues small; some of the

members are greatly interested. We have had few public meetings, but there is quiet preparation for the good seed. The churches, with few exceptions, and the eminently Christian Associations, do not hold out sympathizing hands. How fittingly is the present work called ' New Abolition'! The fetters with which women are bound more degrading, the torture endured more insupportable, than the lash of the taskmaster."

4th mo. 8th, 1877.—"Yesterday I finished the 'Life of Harriet Martineau.' Much as she has been to me for half a century, her strength and goodness were beyond what I had known, her 'sweetness and light' most admirable. I grieve over and rejoice with her by turns."

7th mo. 4th, 1877.—" I attended the Commencement of Cornell University. In the graduating class of near fifty were five women,—co-education. One carried off the highest honors both on class-day and commencement-day, in such wise that we were comforted and able to rejoice in the prospective future of our sex.

" Lord Amberly's 'Analysis of Religious Belief' has especially interested me. How touching his mother's ' Address to the Reader'! His dedication to his wife rivals Stuart Mill's in its beauty and pathos. I place it with that and Lincoln's address at the dedication of the cemetery at Gettysburg,—my trio of gems."

In the Seventh month, 1878, Sarah Pugh went with Lucretia Mott to Rochester, New York, to attend the thirtieth anniversary of the first Woman's Rights Convention. Sarah Pugh was then in her seventy-eighth year, Lucretia Mott in her eighty-fifth. The journey was taken by easy stages, resting with friends by the way, and the meeting was satisfactory to both.

10th mo. 28th, 1878.—"A Boston journal brings the announcement of the death of George Thompson, and with it a touching memorial by W. L. Garrison. Thus our early co-workers pass away. My debt to him is great; he kindled, by his words of fire, my anti-slavery life. My early *principles* were quickened into active participation in the work for that day and hour; a work which has blessed my life and repaid me a hundred-fold. In taking a retrospect the rich experiences loom up brightly before me, shedding light and warmth on my downward path.

"It is, indeed, pleasant to see the sects broadening their platforms and extending their courtesies to one another. The Unitarians holding their convention in a Methodist meeting-house."

4th mo. 27th, 1879.—"Most of the past month I have spent in the house; my first experience, during my life, of comparative helplessness. An unaccountable attack of lumbago compelled me to move about carefully and slowly. The pain is passing away gradually, and I hope to be able ere long to resume my habit of locomotion. . . . My interests are increasingly in the past, with the spirit 'sprightly, joyous, and fragrant;' I will strive to maintain it so to the end."

4th mo. 28th, 1879. (To M. A. Estlin.)—"Our Moral Education Society holds on its way. E. C. Stanton gave us a lecture on 'Womanhood,' which so interested the hearers that they propose having a more public one soon."

In the Fifth month, 1879, Sarah attended the funeral of W. L. Garrison. She writes to an English friend:

7th mo. 4th.—"E. M. Davis and myself arrived in

Boston Fifth mo. 28th, took lunch, and drove directly to the spacious church nearly opposite the Roxbury home. The pulpit was profusely draped with exquisite flowers by a lady artist, who asked to be allowed thus to testify her sympathy and admiration. The seats near were reserved for the family and special friends. The services were all that could be wished, reverential, appreciative, touching. While the throng was taking the last look, the near friends had opportunity to exchange greetings and reminiscences of the loved one. J. G. Whittier was present. The beautiful, quiet cemetery, three miles distant, the perfect day,—as we left the grave the glorious sun setting without a cloud,—all typical of the life that had passed from our midst.

"The Convention of the National Woman Suffrage Association in St. Louis was a success; the advent to the ranks from the South most encouraging. A daughter of Cassius M. Clay from Kentucky; Mrs. Merriwether from Memphis; deep interest felt even in Louisiana. Abounding thanks to Dr. Eliot for his noble work in St. Louis, and for his full sympathy with Woman Suffrage."

12th mo. 31st, 1879.—" My strength is not as of old, though generally able to spend one day in the week in the city, seeing friends or attending meetings. My special interests are ' Woman Suffrage' and ' Moral Education.' The latter society has little to report of outside work, yet the few interested, by tracts and private correspondence, keep it in working order, ready for any special call. Recently E. C. Stanton lectured for us most fittingly on ' Our Girls.' Mrs. S., now sixty-three, has lectured in the West, to large audiences, the past year. Her oldest daughter travels with her. She is specially interested in political subjects and in our South. Among the callers on them here was a Mrs. Saxon from New Orleans. She earnestly wished Mrs. S. and her daughter to go South, where many were prepared to receive their gospel ; she would insure them a warm and courteous reception. She came North to place her sons in school, and to study the machinery of our reform movements. She was familiar with the anti-slavery of the North, and in full sympathy with the leaders."

1st mo. 31*st*, 1880.—"Susan B. Anthony was with us, on her return from attending the Twelfth National Woman Suffrage Convention at Washington ; the best yet held, so report the delegates from here,—two bright young sisters who have lately entered the field, full of interest, enthusiasm, and ability. Some of the friends met at ' Roadside,' where our darling Lucretia Mott was able to spend most of the time with us, sharing in the interest and discussions. Among those who came was the renowned Julia Smith Parker, aged eighty-five ; bright and cheery, delighted to be in the presence and the home of Lucretia Mott, whom she had seen but once, forty years before, in an anti-slavery meeting. She attended in Washington the Suffrage Convention, and a wedding in a Jewish family with whom her translation of the Hebrew Bible had brought her into correspondence. Her childlike simplicity and buoyant, happy nature were charming. While listening to her we could not think of her as old.

"I hope you have received a copy of Mrs. Child's ' Aspirations of the Ages.' What a troubling of waters of late in the spiritual world! Surely many will be healed of their infirmities and comforted.

"I have just read Mrs. Butler's 'St. Catharine of Siena.' At first I wondered why she wrote it; but when she dwelt on the saint's impression of duty to go forth to the world and *publicly* call sinners to repentance, to remonstrate with rulers and people to stay by example and precept the iniquity among them, Mrs. Butler must have felt that she was giving a full vindication of herself in the course to which she has felt called by the same divine voice. What answer can the pious souls who forbid women to speak in the church give to the endorsement of Catharine by the religious world of her time; or those who would limit woman's right to use her gifts, of whatever kind, for the elevation of her race?

"I spent a day and night at Tenafly, the home of E. C. Stanton. We were warmly welcomed to her beautiful *homelike* dwelling, twenty miles from New York, surrounded by forest-trees, almost secluded from the sight of the outside world, yet not from its life and interests. With Mr. Stanton the memorable days of 1840 were pleasantly reviewed; with Mrs. Stanton the past, the present, and the future were themes of great interest, crowded with memories and anticipations. Three of their seven children are with them; Margaret, the married daughter from Iowa, spending the summer. Harriet gone to Berlin with her brother Theodore. Both daughters educated at Vassar. Harriet gives promise, by her talent, culture, and interest in the great questions of the day, to be a worthy worker in the field from which her mother, now sixty-four, feels that she may retire; not that she will retire from earnest work, in writing and attending special meetings. I have given these details as an answer to those who cavil at our devoted laborers running away from their families and life responsibilities. From the days of St. Catharine downward have such censors endeavored to palliate their own apathy and indolence; not that every one should follow in her path, nor even in Sister Dora's, whose work we may wonder at, in all its manifestations of self-abnegation."

11*th mo.* 12*th*, 1880.—"Our beloved and sainted Lucretia Mott has passed from us; to-day I have looked on her worn frame in calm repose, her ample brow showing forth the power once enshrined there.

> 'Spirit, leave thine house of clay!
>   Lingering dust, resign thy breath!
> Spirit, cast thy chains away!
>   Dust, be thou dissolved in death!'

Time's changes thicken around us. L. Maria Child gone suddenly, a few minutes after rising in the morning."

1*st mo.* 7*th*, 1881.—"C. D. Mills's book, 'Oriental Religions,' I have not seen, but am prepared to welcome it, not only from admiration of the author, but from interest in the subject. Oriental life and religions have long had an interest for me; they 'make all men kin,' and humanity is dear to me, but through what different grades does it pass! from the Digger Indians to the Motts, the Garrisons, the Whittiers, and the host of worthies that have shed their hallowed influence over us."

1*st mo.* 30*th*, 1881.—"I spent a day with the family

at ' Roadside,' with E. C. Stanton and S. B. Anthony, on their return from the Washington Convention for Woman Suffrage. A successful one, full of interest and encouragement; a number there that promise to be efficient aids to the movement. New advocates from the West, among them Mrs. Sewall from Indiana; she charmed L. Mott and myself at Rochester by her ability and energy. How comforting it is to find such coming on the stage to take the places of those who have passed away! Lucretia Mott, L. M. Child, George Eliot; even to *read* of them brings joy, to know that such have lived, and that we have been blessed by their ministrations, as will be generations to come. These were themes to dwell upon and recall; our surroundings so instinct with precious memories."

4th mo. 12th, 1881.—" Recently I have assisted our Moral Education Society to distribute many old papers that were on hand, if happily they might contain living seed, which falling on good ground might produce in due season fruit for the healing of the nation. The time seems to have come to proclaim on the house-top things that have been hidden in secret, as if true knowledge would contaminate. Can such teachings as those of the ' Open Letter' and ' Wifehood,' which the Society has reprinted, do harm? The chief work that I can now do is by writing. I attend the meetings to be cheered by the sight of the young and ardent ones who are entering the field of labor."

8th mo. 9th, 1882. (To M. A. Estlin.)—" Yesterday came ' The Shield,' with its report of the ' Repeal Bill.' Brave Mrs. Butler! how one's heart goes out to her and her faithful helpers!

"Since early in the year I have been a decided invalid. After two months' nursing I was able to go down stairs for a few hours, and since then have been slowly gaining strength. 'What ailed you?' Old age. Now near eighty-two, my sight good, I can read much and write a little; outside work has to be turned over to others; there are many able and willing to labor in the reforms of the day. It is a pleasure that I can still aid them by counsel."

In 1882, Sarah Pugh's brother passed away. To him she clung with an ardent sisterly affection. His removal was accepted by her with her usual peaceful serenity.

She remained with her sister-in-law at their residence in Germantown, where she had made her home since 1864. Her sight continued good, much of her time was spent in reading; failure of memory and slowness of apprehension were the chief indications of mental decline.

In the Fourth month, 1884, she fell on the pavement near the house door. This shock to her system produced helplessness and suffering, which she endured without complaint. The gradual weakening of the vital powers continued until the 1st of Eighth month, when she quietly sank to rest.

On the 4th, her friends and relations gathered around her for the last time. Edward Hopper offered an appropriate tribute to her beautiful life, her devoted earnestness in the advocacy of truth, and referred especially to her influence as a teacher upon the character of those placed under her care as pupils.

She was laid by the side of her mother in Fair Hill Cemetery.

www.ingramcontent.com/pod-product-compliance
Lightning Source LLC
Chambersburg PA
CBHW032006010726
47493CB00007B/2291